CHASE ME
The Holmes Brothers Series

Farrah Rochon

Nicobar Press

Copyright © 2017 by Farrah Roybiskie
Cover by Mae Phillips of
CoverFreshDesigns.com

All rights reserved.

ISBN: 978-1-938125-37-9

All characters and events in this book are fictions. Any resemblance to actual persons, living or dead, is strictly coincidental.

Also available in the Holmes Brothers Series:

Deliver Me
Release Me
Rescue Me

CHASE ME
The Holmes Brothers Series

Chapter One

Squinting against the sun's vibrant rays peeking annoyingly through the mahogany custom-made blinds, Indina Holmes executed a full body stretch across the silky 1000 thread count sheets. Her previously tense muscles were now loose and languid after the early morning workout she'd just been subjected to in this bed. Thank God for that particular kind of workout. She'd needed it like a man roaming the desert needed water.

It had been dark when she'd arrived nearly an hour ago, but judging by the dawn's insistent intrusion on her postcoital relaxation, it was past time for her to go.

"I don't want to," Indina half groaned, half whined as her eyes focused on the ceiling fan twirling lazily above her.

You can't stay in this bed all day.

Especially not today, when the culmination of countless meetings, hours of field research, and more time at her design desk than Indina wanted to think about, would finally be put forth before the executive committee responsible for several new federal and state buildings that would be built in the city of New Orleans. Her team's performance today would determine if they landed a billion-dollar contract.

And just like that, the tension was back. Too bad she didn't have time to go for another round between the sheets.

Indina sucked in an uneasy breath as she glanced over at the digital clock on the nightstand.

Shit.

If she didn't get out of here soon she would be late for work. She cursed herself for not bringing her work clothes with her when she left her house earlier this morning.

With one last stretch across the king-size bed, Indina pushed herself up into a sitting position. She could hear the shower's powerful jets coming from just beyond the bathroom door, and cursed herself again. Five minutes in that shower would get rid of the lingering tension in her muscles, with or without the water.

Tossing her legs over the edge of the bed, she walked over to the sitting area and picked up her bra and panties from the chair where she normally dropped them whenever she was here, which had been more often than usual in the past month. Between work and family, her stress levels were at an all-time high. Thank the ever-loving Lord she had a reliable outlet to expend the nervous energy constantly flowing through her bloodstream these days.

Indina slipped her panties on and threaded her arms through the bra's straps, clasping it in the back. Just as she reached for the cotton shirtdress she'd thrown on before coming over, her cell phone rang. She walked back over to where she'd left it on the nightstand, and rolled her eyes when she noticed her brother's name on the screen.

With a sigh, Indina sat on the edge of the bed and swept her thumb across the green button.

"Is there a reason you're calling me before eight a.m.?" she spoke into the phone.

"Good morning to you too," her older brother replied.

She ignored the reprimand in his voice.

"What do you need, Harrison? And there had better be a good reason for you calling me at this time of the morning."

"I need the final head count for the Holmes family reunion cruise. Are you in or are you out? And before you answer that, I want you to think about your newly widowed father and how heartbroken he would be if his only daughter did not participate in this reunion."

She released a disgusted breath. "I hate you so much."

"That was very convincing. It's a good thing I know you don't mean it."

"I mean it," she said.

"Would you just give me the go-ahead to mark you down on the list so I can send the names to the travel agent?" Her brother's harassed voice made her feel marginally better. But only marginally.

Indina massaged the bridge of her nose. She loved her family, but these days she could only take them in small doses. She visited her dad at least once during the week—even more if she could—and tried to make as many Sunday dinners as possible, but that was only a few hours out of her day, and once her brothers started eating, there was very little talking. Could she survive being stuck on a cruise ship with them for three days without going straight-up insane?

And it wasn't limited to her pesky brothers this time around. The entire Holmes clan would be there. Her late Uncle Wesley's three sons, Alexander, Elijah and Tobias, along with their wives and their ever-growing brood of children were all going. And if her boys would be there, Indina knew her Aunt Margo would be there too, along with her husband, Gerald Mitchell.

There would be Holmeses galore. That poor cruise ship had no idea what it was in store for.

"Indina!" Harrison's voice startled her. "Are you coming on the cruise or not? Wait, let me rephrase that. Are you going to break your father's heart or not?"

"Stop it with the guilt trip."

"I'm just saying."

"I've never been on a cruise before," she pointed out. "What if I get seasick?"

"You can wear one of those patches behind your ear. And if that doesn't work there's medicine you can take," Harrison said. "I'll tell

Eli to bring you some."

Great. That's what she got for having a cousin who was a doctor, and who also happened to be married to a doctor.

"You got any more excuses you need me to shoot down before I head to my office?" her brother asked.

"I really do hate you right now," Indina said. She rubbed her temple as she came to terms with the fact that there was no way out of this. "Fine, I'll come on the damn cruise."

"I'd already marked you down as a yes," Harrison replied. "I just called to make sure *you* knew that you were going."

"Asshole," she said.

"I love you too. By the way, I put you in the cabin with Lily and Jasmine."

"Lily and Jasmine?" Indina sat up straight. "You do realize I'm forty-two years old, don't you? Why would I want to room with a couple of teenagers?"

No, make that a teenager and a pre-teen. Her cousin Alex's daughter, Jasmine, was only twelve.

"Because everyone else is paired up and the cabin rates are based on double occupancy," he explained. "If I didn't put you in the girls' room you'd have to pay an upcharge because you're a single."

A single. As if it was some kind of diseased designation she wore on her chest.

"And just why would you think I would be

alone?" Indina asked.

"Why wouldn't I?" The incredulousness in his voice made her want to slap him through the phone. "When was the last time you brought anyone around?"

Indina ignored that question. It had been nearly two years since she'd been in a bring-him-over-to-meet-the-family kind of relationship. That didn't mean her brother had to throw it in her face. Just for that, she would pluck his insensitive ass right between the eyebrows next time she saw him.

"I won't have the cabin for myself," Indina said. "I'm bringing someone."

"Who?" Harrison asked.

"None of your business."

"I need the name for the travel agent."

"I'll text you the name later. Now leave me alone. I need to get going."

The shower stopped the minute she disconnected the call. Moments later, the bathroom door opened and Griffin Sims walked out, wiping his face with a plush cranberry-colored towel. There was another towel wrapped around his waist, hanging low on his hips. His chiseled dark brown chest glistened with specks of moisture. Indina tracked a water droplet that traveled down his torso to the smattering of curly hair that trailed from his belly button to below the towel.

She pulled her bottom lip between her teeth and damn near whimpered.

Griffin stopped short when he spotted her. "You're still here?"

"I'm sorry," Indina said, rising from where she'd sat on the edge of his bed. "I got a phone call that I had to take just as I started getting dressed."

"No need to apologize. It's just that you're usually gone by the time I get out of the shower."

Her eyes roamed over his muscular back and shoulders as he walked over to the dresser. She didn't know where he found the time to go to the gym, but she appreciated the way he took care of his body.

"Are you still nervous about today?" Griffin asked.

He turned to her, holding the pair of heather gray boxer briefs he'd retrieved from the dresser. He dropped the towel and Indina couldn't hold back the whimper this time.

She had explored the heavy weight between his legs with her tongue just an hour ago, yet her mouth still watered at the sight of it. She just stood there and marveled at his beauty as he pulled the briefs up his well-toned legs.

"Indina," Griffin called.

She blinked several times. "Wait. What?"

A knowing grin curled up the side of his mouth. "I asked if you were still nervous about today?"

"A little, but at least I'm no longer tense."

"Happy I could help with that," he said. His

deep chuckle reverberated along her nerve endings, straight down to that spot between her legs he'd pleasured this morning.

Over the last eight months, she'd relied on Griffin for that particular kind of pleasurable help on a regular basis. They'd met a little over a year ago, when Indina decided to move away from residential interior design and concentrate on the more lucrative industrial sector. She began freelancing with the structural engineering firm where Griffin worked after one of the owners sought her out.

Griffin was the lead engineer on the very first project she worked on with Sykes-Wilcox. The physical attraction had been there from the moment she walked into a conference room and saw him braced over a set of blueprints, his shirtsleeves rolled up on his strong arms. Indina decided not to act on that attraction until several months later, after she learned through the office grapevine that Griffin was divorced and not necessarily looking for a relationship.

She knew all about that. Not the being divorced part, but being burnt out on relationships?

Hell yes, she knew about that.

But there were only so many *Top Ten Self-Pleasuring Tips* articles a girl could be expected to read. And she'd read them. *All* of them. She needed the real deal. The way Indina saw it she and Griffin were in the perfect position to provide each other with some much needed sexual relief.

She could still remember how her fingers had trembled as she'd typed the text, asking Griffin if he was up for a little casual, no-strings-attached sex. She wasn't sure how she would have handled working with him if he had turned down her bold invitation to meet her at the Bourbon Orleans Hotel in the French Quarter.

He'd arrived at the hotel even before she did, and with that one afternoon, they'd embarked upon a coworkers with benefits arrangement that never failed to leave her body satisfied and her mind free of relationship drama.

Her phone beeped. It was a text from Harrison with the travel agent's name and phone number, and a reminder to send the name of the person who would be sharing her cabin.

Indina looked over at Griffin. He'd just put on a gingham blue dress shirt, but hadn't bothered to button it up yet. Her mouth watered again at the expanse of exposed skin.

He looked up from the neckties he'd been contemplating.

"Everything okay?" he asked.

Indina nodded and decided not to ask the question that had been on the tip of her tongue. Hadn't she just acknowledged that what she and Griffin had going was perfect? Why would she jeopardize it by asking him to come with her on this damn cruise?

She slipped her dress over her head, then

picked up her wristlet and keys from where she'd dropped them on the dresser.

In a real relationship this is where they would kiss each other goodbye. But this wasn't a real relationship. It wasn't how she and Griffin rolled.

And that was just fine with her.

"See you in a few hours," Indina said, gripping the handle on the bedroom door. "I'll lock the front door on my way out."

"As you can see, ladies and gentlemen, our design balances both style and efficiency, all within the small footprint available for the new office complex," the lead architect, Jason Leblanc, said as he rounded the table. He gestured to Griffin. "Next."

Griffin pointed the remote at the miniature display model in the center of the conference room table and pressed the button. Images of people sitting in a glass-enclosed lobby projected onto the display's stark white walls. It had been Indina's idea to incorporate the projected images into the presentation, giving the officials from the city planning commission, along with the executives from his engineering firm, a virtual tour of the new state office building they were bidding on.

Months of work had gone into this project. If they landed it, it would be the largest contract

Sykes-Wilcox Engineering had ever scored. Not only did it include building new government buildings in the city of New Orleans, but because it was in conjunction with the state, there would be projects all over south Louisiana.

Knowing that everything came down to this presentation should have been enough to force him to concentrate on what was being discussed around the table. Yet, Griffin's mind continued to wander to the woman sitting at the far end of the conference room.

Indina sat with her hands folded on the table, her expression cool and collected. If she was still nervous, she was doing a kickass job hiding it. Not that Griffin expected anything different from her. When it came to her job, Indina's mantra was *never let them see you sweat*. She was the consummate professional. It was sexy as hell.

As Jason finished up his portion of the presentation, he said, "I will now turn things over to my colleague, Indina Holmes, who will go into further detail about how we've incorporated sustainable environmentally-friendly interior design into the structure."

As Indina rose from her seat, it took all Griffin had within him to focus on the words she was saying instead of that ridiculously gorgeous mouth. That mouth was more of a mystery to him than anything else. He'd only kissed it twice, and never for more than a couple of seconds. Yet he'd kissed other parts of her body untold times over the past eight months. In fact, just this morning her soft thighs had cushioned his head as he'd explored between her legs with his tongue.

Shit!

Griffin surreptitiously sucked in a swift breath. How in the hell was he supposed to think about anything else now?

"A key directive we received when we were presented with this project was to go green, and I'm proud to say that, once completed, this entire structure will not only reach current LEED gold-certified standards, but will surpass the code required by the Department of Energy. In fact, it will be one of the greenest buildings in the southeastern quadrant," Indina said.

She nodded at him and Griffin clicked the remote again, illuminating another room on the 3-D model.

"One of the most ingenious aspects of the design is the on-site fitness center."

"Wait a minute," the commission member with the snowy Santa Claus beard interrupted. "An on-site fitness center? That's a job perk that goes above and beyond what the city can or even should provide, don't you think?"

"Not when you consider the number of days of lost productivity due to illnesses associated with obesity, diabetes and other diseases," Indina said. "This on-site gym encourages a healthy lifestyle for government employees.

"But this is so much more than just a fitness

center, ladies and gentlemen. The recumbent bikes, treadmills and elliptical machines all feed into the main power system. As employees exercise, they will also help to generate electricity for the building, thus saving the state money in the long run."

That got everyone's attention. Several of the people around the table sat up in their chairs and peered closer at the design.

"That's genius," the head of the city planning commission said.

"Thank our lead structural engineer. It was his idea." Indina smiled at Griffin. "It's all yours."

"Thank you." He winked at her as he walked to the head of the table where she'd been standing, then he closed out the presentation by wrapping up the points Indina and Jason had already made.

"You mind hitting the lights?" Griffin asked Jason.

He waited until their architect turned the lights in the conference room back on before concluding the meeting with one final pitch about the benefits of a long-term relationship between Sykes-Wilcox and local government.

"This property is just the beginning," Griffin said. "As advancements are made in clean energy and green technology, we can reduce Louisiana's carbon footprint and be an example for the rest of the country. Sykes-Wilcox's partnership with the city of New Orleans has the potential to turn this city into one others around the world will want to emulate."

His anxiety slowly lessened as he surveyed the room. There were actual smiles on their faces as the city leaders enthusiastically discussed the presentation. Griffin shook the hands of each member of the city planning commission as they exited the room, then turned to his boss.

"How was that, Mark?" Griffin asked.

"Phenomenal," Mark Sykes answered. "A simply phenomenal presentation. I felt pretty confident about landing this contract before, but after what you and your team just did, I have no doubts it's ours."

"I thought it was your job to manage expectations," Griffin asked with a laugh.

"No need. This contract is in the bag. Now if only I can convince Ms. Holmes here to join Sykes-Wilcox full time, my day will be complete," he said, motioning for Indina to join them.

"You can forget that," Griffin said. "From what I've seen, she spends most of her day turning down offers from other architectural firms trying to lure her to join them."

"Are you two talking about me?" Indina asked as she sidled up next to Mark.

"Yes, we are," his boss said. "I was just telling Griffin that it's time for you to stop toying with us and just get on the payroll at Sykes-Wilcox already. You, Griffin and Jason make a dynamic team."

"I think today's presentation proves that I don't have to be on the payroll in order to be a part of this dynamic team," Indina said.

Mark wagged his finger at her. "Be careful with this one, Griff. She's sharp."

"That she is," Griffin said. "Which is why I'm content with having her any way I can get her." He paused just long enough to catch Indina narrowing her eyes at him. "On our team," Griffin finished.

"You're right about that," Mark said. "Sykes-Wilcox is happy to pay your steep hourly rate, Ms. Holmes. Anything to keep this team together."

"I am very satisfied with our contractual relationship," Indina said. "I have no intentions of going anywhere else."

"Now *that's* what I want to here," Mark said. He tapped them both on the back. "Good job today. You too, Jason. You all need to take the rest of the day off and go out to celebrate."

"Only if we get to use the company credit card," Griffin replied.

"You always have to go that extra step, don't you?" Mark said with a laugh. The moment his boss walked away, Griffin turned to Indina and hooked a thumb back toward Mark. He spoke before she did, not wanting to give her the chance to call him on his earlier comment about having her any way he could get her. He knew he'd toed the line with that one, just as he'd done with that wink he'd given her earlier.

Public displays of affection were not welcomed.

"In the four years I've worked for him, I've never seen Mark so infatuated," Griffin said. "Not that I can blame him. You were in rock star mode throughout the entire presentation. Congratulations."

"Thank you," she said. "Normally, I'd say it's too early for congratulations, but based on the commission members' reactions, I think Mark is right. This one is in the bag."

"Of course it's in the bag. We kicked ass today."

"We did, didn't we?" She thrust her hand out to him. "Nice work."

Griffin glanced at her hand, and then brought his eyes back to hers. "Do you remember how many hours we put into this? What we accomplished here today at least warrants a congratulatory hug, doesn't it?"

"Griffin?" she hedged.

He lowered his voice. "C'mon, Indina. I know we have this no PDAs in the workplace rule, but what's a simple hug after all the work we did on this project?"

She hesitated for just a moment before stepping into his embrace. The awkward, impersonal hug completely gutted him. He barely had the chance to feel her against him before she backed away and mumbled something about going over to help Jason pack up the 3-D model.

Griffin studied her as she walked over to the

conference table. Even after all these months together, he had no idea what to make of her.

Just a few hours ago he'd been buried deep inside her. He'd licked his way around her body, from that piece of heaven between her thighs, up to her soft, slightly rounded belly, and her full, delectable breasts. She'd done the same to him. So why was it so damn hard for her to show him any kind of affection outside of the bedroom?

The better question was, why was he surprised? That's the way things had always been between him and Indina.

Back when they'd first started this no-strings-attached thing, they'd both been in a place where a real relationship just didn't fit in with their lifestyles. But things had changed for Griffin over the last few months. The emotionless hook-ups—while physically gratifying as hell—just weren't enough for him anymore. He wanted more.

Indina, unfortunately, did not.

She'd told him so from the very beginning, and she hadn't given any indication that her feelings had changed regarding their relationship—or whatever one called this arrangement between them.

Indina had her own name for it. They were fuck buddies. Plain and simple.

It was hard for Griffin to accept that this was all they would ever be to each other, but he also wasn't stupid enough to jeopardize what they had going just because he wanted more than

Indina was willing to give. That's why whenever that text popped up on his phone, asking if he wanted to get together, he kept his mouth shut and just enjoyed it. Great sex was great sex, and if he could get that with a beautiful woman a couple times a week, he was ahead of most of the single guys he knew.

So what if that beautiful woman couldn't bring herself to kiss him on the lips?

A familiar ache slammed into Griffin's chest.

He hadn't realized just how meaningful a simple kiss was to him until the moment it registered that he and Indina had never really kissed. For months they'd engaged in every carnal act known to man, but not when it came to that most basic form of intimacy. He craved it. To have her open her mouth and let him inside—it would mean everything to him.

But that wasn't the way they operated.

They got each other off. Period. And once they were out of bed, there was no talk about what went on behind closed doors. As far as anyone else knew, they were coworkers and nothing more.

Griffin told himself he was okay with that, but lately, thoughts of Indina eventually finding a guy she *was* willing to kiss had been keeping him up at night. Even though, as far as he knew, she hadn't so much as looked at another guy since they'd been together, there had never been a discussion about exclusivity. What if she suddenly decided she was ready to test the dating waters again? What would he do if one day that text message wasn't about hooking up, but instead was news that she'd met someone else? Just the thought sent a rush of anguish spiraling through him.

Griffin knew he was on borrowed time. Indina would eventually want a relationship. And he couldn't pretend he was okay with that being with anyone but him.

Timing was key. If he told her how he felt about her before she was ready to consider taking that next step, he could risk messing up what they had going here. But if he stuck with the status quo, he ran the risk of some other guy coming in and sweeping her off her feet. He couldn't just sit back and allow that to happen either.

He looked over at the conference table. Jason had just zipped up the case he'd used to transport the model. Indina stood off to the side. She was frowning at her phone.

Griffin was at her side in three strides. "Is everything okay?" he asked.

Her head popped up. "What?"

He motioned to her phone. "Everything okay?"

"Oh, yeah." She waved off any concern. "Just my brother nagging me again." She looked down at the phone, then back up at him. Her brow dipped.

"What is it?" Griffin asked.

"No." She shook her head. "Never mind.

You're going to think I'm crazy."

"Try me."

She hesitated for a moment before releasing an exasperated breath. "I understand that this is an outrageous request and I don't blame you if you say no."

"Indina, would you come on with it?"

"Okay, fine. Here's the deal. This coming weekend is the annual Holmes Family Reunion. This year they've decided to hold it on a three-day cruise to Mexico." She bit her bottom lip as she looked up at him. "I need a plus one."

Griffin's head snapped back.

She held her hands up. "Like I said, I know this is outrageous. And I'll pay for your cruise, of course. It's just that the room is double occupancy, and the friend who I thought would be able to come with me won't be able to make it. And the chances of me finding someone who can come along at the last minute are slim. And—"

"Indina!" Griffin stopped her. "Yes."

Her eyes blinked several times in rapid succession. "Yes? You'll do it?"

Three days on a cruise ship with her? Hell yeah he was down for that.

"When do we leave?" Griffin asked.

Her entire body seemed to wilt with relief. "Friday afternoon," she answered with a grateful smile.

Griffin couldn't stop his own smile from forming. She didn't know it yet, but she'd just given him the opportunity he'd been hoping for. If he couldn't convince Indina that they should be together while they spent three days sharing a cabin on a cruise ship, then maybe he didn't deserve her after all. But Griffin knew he most definitely deserved her. They deserved each other. He couldn't wait to show her.

"Thank you so much," Indina said. "You just saved me from having to eat crow spoon fed from my brother. And remember, this is my treat. Consider it the celebration for getting through this presentation."

"I'm all for celebrating, but you're not paying for my cruise," Griffin said. "If anything it should be the other way around. Using that image projector on the 3-D model was a huge hit. That was all you."

A blush formed on her soft brown cheeks. She seemed to feed off the praise he heaped upon her body in the bedroom, but for some reason that didn't extend to accepting compliments at work.

She gave him a casual shrug. "I guess you're right."

"I know I am."

It was on the tip of his tongue to ask her out to dinner tonight to celebrate their big day. But he and Indina didn't *do* dinner. The closest they'd come to an actual dinner date—outside of a few casual Friday get-togethers for drinks and half-priced appetizers with the rest of their work team—was eating leftover Chinese from his fridge one night when she'd had to wait out a rainstorm after sex.

It was that same night, when he couldn't convince her to stay at his place, that Griffin first recognized just how much his feelings for her had changed. And how he couldn't go on with the way things were.

He was no longer satisfied being Indina's friend with benefits. He needed more. He needed to be the man in her life. He needed to be the one she shared more than just her body with. He needed her heart.

He had to let her know how he felt about her. And with the invitation to join her on this cruise, she'd just given him the perfect opportunity to tell her.

Now he just had to figure out how to go about doing that without scaring her away.

Indina paid for forty minutes on the parking meter before tucking the receipt on her dashboard and crossing Gravier Street. She'd been smart enough to call Mackenna Arnold before assuming her old college roommate was in her office at City Hall. It was a good thing she did. Today was Mack's day to hold office hours at the Arts Council of New Orleans, where she volunteered as a pro bono attorney for struggling artists, musicians and writers in need of legal help.

Indina entered the lobby of The Exchange Centre, the downtown high-rise that housed the Arts Council, and took the elevator to the eighth floor. She greeted Elizabeth, the receptionist, as she entered the office suite and pointed toward the hallway.

"Is she free?" Indina asked.

The receptionist looked at her computer. "For the next hour. She has a late appointment coming in at six."

"Thanks, Liz." Indina made her way to the small office at the end of the hallway. The various attorneys who volunteered at the Arts Council all shared it, coming in on various days, one to two times a week.

Knocking softly, she pushed the door open to find Mack on the phone. Her friend held up a finger as she continued her conversation.

"A client just walked through the door. We'll have to continue this at a later date," Mack said to whoever was on the other end of the call. She jammed her finger at the touchscreen and set the cell phone on the desk.

"Thank God you came in," Mack said, slouching forward until her forehead hit the stack of files that sat in front of her.

"Do I even want to know?" Indina asked.

"No, you don't," came her friend's muffled voice. Mack raised her head and pushed back from the desk, walking over to Indina and enveloping her in a hug. "You're looking fabulous as always. Let me just start by saying that I am *so* sorry I can't go on this cruise with you. I swear if I didn't have a dozen things to do this weekend I would be there. I need a vacation more than I need air."

"I know you do," Indina said. "That's why you were the first person I asked. We'll have to plan a girls' weekend as soon as you can get some time off."

Mack rolled her eyes. "As if that's going to happen anytime soon."

"You have to slow down, Mack. I don't have to remind you how quickly burnout happens."

"I know, I know," her friend said. "Eventually. Oh, and I have to apologize for cancelling dinner the other night. *Again.* There was an emergency meeting in the 7th Ward over the school voucher program."

Indina waved that off. "You don't have to keep apologizing. You think I don't know how busy your life is these days? Between practicing law, teaching and the city council, I don't know where you find the time to eat or sleep."

"I don't get much of either, but I'm trying to do better. I promise not to cancel next time."

"It's all good," Indina said. "I had some pho and spring rolls delivered from that new Vietnamese place down the street and ate it in my pajamas while watching TV. It's my own version of Netflix and chill."

Mack held up a hand. "Please don't use that phrase. I thought it meant actually chilling out and watching TV, so I invited the group of law students we have working here over to my place to celebrate after finishing a big case."

"You didn't," Indina said.

"Yes, I did. Sent a group text asking them all to come Netflix and chill. Next thing I know, it's all over Snap Chat that there's an orgy going down at Councilwoman Arnold's house."

Indina burst out laughing. "That's what happens when you have no teenagers in your life to keep you posted on the latest slang."

"Next time you have Liliana over, call me. I'll pay her to give me lessons. I'd rather not have horny law students showing up at my place with pockets full of condoms." Mack settled her backside against the desk. "Although, if I didn't think it would get blasted all over social media, I would have slept with one of them. It would be nice to finally have an orgasm that wasn't self-induced."

"Now *that* would be a reason to celebrate," Indina said, taking a seat on one of the mismatched chairs in the cramped office.

"Speaking of celebrations, please tell me that one's in order after today's presentation?" Mack asked.

Being on the City Council, Indina and Mackenna had set boundaries once Indina began working on city contracts. Neither of them wanted people thinking that Mack had shown any kind of favoritism just because they were sorority sisters with a friendship that had lasted over twenty years. But Indina knew her friend was always in her corner.

"We won't know for certain until all bids are in, but we kicked ass today. They were riveted."

Mack held up a hand for a high-five. "Gimme some."

Indina slapped her palm then settled back in the chair and folded her hands over her stomach.

"Now, why don't you tell me what that call was all about," she said, gesturing to the phone.

Mack rolled her eyes as she pushed away from the desk and went back around it, sitting in the worn leather desk chair. "My ex-husband being a pain in my ass yet again," she answered.

"Seriously? The divorce has been final for nearly a year. Why is he still being difficult?"

"Because he lives to be difficult," Mack said. "He's still pissed that I got his precious boat in the divorce settlement and that it's just sitting there unused. I told him that I'd sell it to him, but I'm not giving him shit."

"If it was anyone but Carter I'd say just give him the boat to get him out of your hair, but he'd just find some other reason to hound you."

"He's not getting the boat. Other than the condo, which was rightfully mine anyway, that boat is the only other thing I got out of that marriage."

Indina still couldn't believe how badly her friend had been shafted in her divorce settlement, but it shouldn't be a surprise, seeing as Carter Arnold was one of the most successful divorce lawyers in the south. If Indina wasn't already sour on relationships, the hell Mack had been through over this past year would have been enough to make her run away screaming. Who the hell needed that kind of drama in their lives?

Not her. She was done chasing after love.

Her friend leaned back in her chair and crossed her stockinged feet on the desk. "That's what I get for not taking your advice in the first place," Mack said. "I should have listened when you told me Carter wasn't worth my time."

"You were twenty-five years old and dick sprung. You weren't listening to anyone's advice." Indina hunched her shoulders. "Look at the bright side; it wasn't always bad. You and Carter had some good years in the beginning."

"No we didn't," Mack said. "I spent the first three years working to get us both through law school and the next twelve helping him to build his practice. That was never a marriage. It was a business partnership with good sex thrown in about once a week. And toward the end even that wasn't good. I got the three strokes and I'm out treatment. He saved all his best moves for Becky with the good hair."

Indina grimaced. "I heard they're getting married," she said of the paralegal that Mack's ex-husband had an affair with.

Mack huffed. "As if I care. As long as it keeps his shady ass out of my life, I'm happy."

But she wasn't. Indina had sensed it in her friend over the past year. She was grateful that

Mack had finally ended her toxic marriage, but hated that it had all happened in such a high profile manner. But when two well-known figures were embroiled in a nasty divorce, it was bound to cause tongues to wag.

Carter Arnold was probably one of the best-known faces in New Orleans. His fake smile adorned dozens of billboards around the city and his stale commercials flooded the late-night TV spots. When Mackenna won her seat on the city council, the two became one of the city's most high-powered couples. When their marriage ended in a blaze of glory following Carter's infidelity, it became fodder for every gossip blog covering local news.

"I so wish you could come on the cruise this weekend," Indina said. "I don't know anyone who deserves a vacation more than you do."

"Tell me about it." Mack rolled her eyes, then her brow furrowed. "What made you change your mind? Last time we talked, you were adamant about not going on the cruise yourself."

"I caved to my annoying brother. Harrison called this morning and laid a guilt trip on me. Said I should think about Dad and how he would feel if I didn't show up."

"That was low, but apparently effective, so score one for Harrison."

"He's the pain in *my* ass," Indina said.

"Oh, stop. You're going to get on that cruise ship and forget about everything happening back here on land. Damn, I'm jealous."

"You can still join us. I'm sure we can find a cabin for you somewhere."

"Do you no longer have a spot in your room?"

Indina pulled her bottom lip between her teeth. She and Mack were best friends, but she hadn't shared that she was getting it on with one of her coworkers.

"Uh, no. Griffin is coming with me." She hoped that sounded as casual as she'd intended.

Mack's forehead dipped even more with her frown. "Griffin? The engineer with the nice ass who worked on the Toussaint project with you?"

"I thought they hadn't decided yet who the new museum would be named after?" Indina asked.

"It will be named after Toussaint," Mack assured her. It had been Mackenna's idea to name the new museum celebrating New Orleans's rich musical history after Allan Toussaint. The late musician had been one of the city's best music ambassadors. "Is that the guy you're talking about?"

Indina nodded. "That's him. He's been the lead on the last three projects I've done with Sykes-Wilcox."

"And you're sharing a room with him? It sounds to me like you two have been doing more than just working." She said it jokingly, but when Indina didn't respond Mack's eyes grew wide. "Are you?"

"We are," Indina admitted, caving yet again to pressure.

"You're dating? I can't believe you didn't tell me you were dating someone."

"We're not necessarily dating. We're just…umm." Indina bit her bottom lip. She lowered her voice and hunched forward. "Look, Griffin and I are fuck buddies, alright?"

Mack's brow nearly touched her hairline. She screeched. "For how long, bitch?"

"Is that the way you address all of your constituents?"

"For. How. Long. Bitch?"

"About eight months," Indina said with a laugh.

Mack stared at her, slack-jawed and shaking her head. "I can't believe you didn't tell me. Some kind of friend you are. You know it's been a while since I had some. I count on my friends to let me live vicariously through them." She sat back in her chair and folded her hands over her stomach. "Don't hold back. I want details. *Explicit* details."

"Eww, no. I'm not giving you details," Indina said. "There aren't really any details to share."

"There hell there aren't."

"Honestly, Mack, it's nothing to fuss over. We get together, we have sex, we go about our business."

"But you work together almost every day."

She shrugged. "Doesn't matter. We don't

discuss what we do in the bedroom anywhere but in the bedroom." She held her hands up. "I'm only doing what men do all the time. How many times have I been just a piece of ass for a guy?"

"So is that all he is? A piece of ass?"

"No. Not really."

Well, maybe.

But Indina didn't think of Griffin that way. She wasn't using him in the same way he wasn't using here. Their relationship was mutually beneficial.

"I don't consider him a piece of ass, but when I think about it, I guess he is." She shrugged. "I've played that role enough times in my life to know."

"This is the part where I'm probably supposed to tell you that all men are not like your old boyfriends and you should give Griffin a chance," Mack said. "But after the phone call I just had with my ex I'm ready to kill all men, so Griffin is on his own."

"Griffin and I are exactly what we need to be to each other—sexual relief," Indina said. "Nothing more."

"I have to admit I'm jealous," Mack said. "I'd kill for my own personal Dial-A-Dick service."

Indina nearly choked on her laugh. "Isn't that what most of the dating apps are these days?"

"Can you imagine the talk it would stir up if

my face showed up in a dating app? *Carter Arnold prepares to marry his mistress while Council Member Arnold searches for single male with good teeth and no criminal record."*

"Is that what we're down to when it comes to dating criteria, good teeth and no record?"

"I'll even take dental implants," Mack said. "But you can forget about getting me on a dating website." She swiped a finger over the film of dust on the desk and brushed it off. "I'll have to be satisfied with my ever-growing collection of sex toys. I've tried so many that I had to start storing them in a second drawer."

"You can always send another Netflix and chill invite to the cute law student." Indina winked as she rose from her chair. "I need to get going. Now that I'm going on this cruise, I need to head to the mall for clothes to wear. And a swimsuit," she said with a grimace.

"Get a two-piece."

"Maybe if I'd kept up my gym membership."

"Cut that shit out. You look fabulous," Mack said, coming from behind the desk again.

"I can say the same about you," Indina said. She gave her friend a hug. "Call that college student," she whispered.

"I just picked up a bulk-size pack of batteries from Costco. I'm good for the next few months. Oh, before you go, " Mack said, shutting the door Indina had just opened and leaning against it. "Can you please speak to your brother? I need him to stop harassing me."

Indina's chin dropped to her chest. "What did Ezra do this time?"

"He was at my office in City Hall on Monday, hounding my assistant about the new company that took over the garbage collection for the French Quarter. My office has told him more than once that I have no dealings with BGF Disposal, yet he still insists that I'm hiding something. He needs to get a freaking life."

"I'm sorry, Mack. He's been freelancing ever since he was let go from the paper. He's convinced if he can find a huge story he'll get picked up by a national magazine."

"He needs new methods of investigating. All he's doing now is trying to find a story where there isn't one. Tell him if he keeps coming around I'm going to have him arrested."

"I'll talk to him," Indina said. "I promise." She gave her friend another hug. "I probably won't see you until after I get back from the cruise. Let's try to get together sometime next week."

"Yes. I promise not to cancel this time." Mack opened the office's door. "Oh, and remember to bring sunscreen. Don't believe that bullshit about black people not being able to get sunburn. It's a crock."

"I will," Indina said with a laugh.

"And don't do anything I wouldn't do," Mack said. "*Today* Me, not *College* Me."

"But College You had so much more fun,"

Indina said.

"Fine, go on and be College Me. As long as you tell me all about it when you get back."

Indina looked over her shoulder and winked. "You got it."

Chapter Two

Griffin turned into the parking garage on Erato Street and, after getting his ticket from the attendant, pulled into the first available spot he came across. He grabbed his bag from the trunk and quickly made his way across the street to the cruise terminal. God, he hated running late.

He'd left his Uptown house a half hour ago, thinking he'd give himself extra time to make the fifteen-minute drive from Lowerline Avenue to the port. He hadn't factored in catching every single traffic light, or getting stuck behind a slow-moving garbage truck.

Griffin tried to tamp down the nervousness that had begun collecting in his gut this morning, when he realized he would meet Indina's family today. On the one hand it shouldn't matter what her family thought about him. He and Indina weren't even officially a couple.

Yet, that's exactly what he was hoping would come of this weekend. If he could convince Indina to turn this no-strings-attached thing they had going into something more serious, her family's impression of him would mean a helluva lot.

Griffin spotted her standing among a bunch of chattering adults and kids gathered in the area just before the security checkpoint.

Damn. Coming from a relatively small family, he hadn't expected *this* many people. He walked up to the crowd of Holmeses.

"Uh, hello."

It was as if he hadn't spoken at all.

"Hello," Griffin said again, a bit louder this time.

The chatter stopped and two dozen sets of curious eyes turned to him. He suddenly felt like a bug under a microscope.

It didn't take a degree in rocket science for him to figure out that Indina probably hadn't told her family that he would be joining them on the cruise. By the looks being directed his way, not only did the Holmeses not know he would be attending their family reunion, they didn't know about him. Period.

"You made it," Indina said, breaking away from the pack and coming to stand next to him. She turned to her family. "Everyone, this is Griffin Sims. Griffin this is way too many people to name at the moment. I'll introduce you to everyone once we've boarded the ship."

"Which we need to do right now," a guy with Indina's hazel-colored eyes said. He held his hand out to him. "I'm Harrison; her brother," he said, tilting his head toward Indina. "Glad to have you on board."

"Thanks," Griffin said.

"Okay, let's get going," Harrison said.

Several of her family members came over to greet him as they all made their way toward the security line. Their smiles seemed genuine, if a bit curious.

This was going better than Griffin had expected. Maybe it was a good thing he'd arrived at the last minute. It didn't leave much time for Indina's family to question the new guy. Of course, he would be on a cruise ship with them for three days. There would be plenty time for questions.

One guy, who looked as if he ate linebackers for lunch, introduced himself as Indina's baby brother, Reid.

"So, how do you know Dennie?" Reid ask as he hefted his bag onto the conveyor belt.

"We're coworkers," Griffin answered.

"Coworkers, huh? What kind of work do you do?"

"None of your business," Indina interjected. "And if you call me Dennie again I'm going to hurt you."

"I was just trying to make conversation," Reid said. "Stop being so damn testy."

"Stop being so damn nosy."

"Okay, what are we fighting about now?" An older gentleman stepped up to where they'd gathered just past the security checkpoint.

"Indina's being her old mean self again," Reid said.

"And this one is being a pest, as usual," Indina returned.

"Neither of you are too old for timeout," the man, who must have been Indina's dad, said.

"Old man, stop pretending you know anything about timeout," Reid said. He hooked a thumb toward his father. "This one gave more whippings than anyone else on the block."

"And I'm sure if I looked hard enough I could find a switch for you right now," he said.

Indina burst out laughing. "Griffin, this is my dad, Clark Holmes. Dad, this is my coworker, Griffin Sims." She gave her father a kiss on the cheek. "And, for the record, I never once got a whipping."

Reid grunted as he moved toward the front of the line of Holmeses preparing to board the ship.

If not for the head of gray hair, Griffin would have thought Clark Holmes was too young to have a daughter in her forties. He was solidly built, with muscles that bunched underneath the sleeves of his polo shirt, much like his two sons Griffin had met already this afternoon.

He took Clark's proffered hand and noted the strength in his grip.

"Nice to meet you," the older man said. "Happy to have you along for the reunion." With that, Indina's father continued on with the rest of the family as they made their way across a Plexiglas-enclosed gangway.

Griffin caught the hem of Indina's shirt and tugged, stunting her progress.

She looked back at him with a frown. "What?"

"Did anyone in your family even know I was coming along?" Griffin whispered.

"Uh, no," she said. "Well, my brother, Harrison, knew I was bringing someone. He just didn't know who."

"You didn't think it would be better to let everyone know in advance?"

"Do you see how many people are here? There's twenty-five total, not including the two of us. How was I even supposed to let them know?"

"Email?" he suggested with a shrug. "Or maybe an old-fashioned phone call?"

Indina snorted. "Yeah, right. Look, just relax and enjoy the weekend. Well, as much as you can relax around this crew. Watch what you say. My family can be a bit…well…nosy."

"Oh, nice," he said.

"It'll be fine." Indina grabbed his arm and pulled him along. "Come on. According to my cousin, Toby, there's a huge buffet as soon as we board the ship. I skipped breakfast this morning and I am *starving*."

They filed onto the ship, and were directed to the lido deck, which did indeed have the biggest buffet Griffin had ever seen in his thirty-eight years on planet Earth. He loaded his plate with peel-and-eat shrimp, and settled at one of the four tables Indina's cousins managed to commandeer for them. An older woman, who'd introduced herself as Indina's Aunt Margo, sat at the table with them. She explained that she was a Holmes by marriage, having been married to Indina's late uncle, Wesley.

A few minutes later, a man Griffin recognized, but couldn't quite place, set a plate in front of Margo and took the seat next to her. She introduced him as her husband, Gerald Mitchell, and the light bulb in Griffin's head instantly went off. Gerald Mitchell was one of the top lawyers in New Orleans. He frequently appeared on the local evening news whenever there was a high-profile case that warranted commentary.

As they ate, they chatted about the upcoming football season, debating the Saints' chances of making it to the playoffs. Griffin learned soon after moving to New Orleans seven years ago that Saints football was a topic of utmost importance, and that *everyone* had an opinion on it.

He eyed the buffet stations, but after all the shrimp he'd just inhaled, Griffin knew he wouldn't be able to fit in anything else. Indina's younger brother didn't seem to have that problem. Griffin stopped counting after Reid's third visit to the buffet. He figured the guy either hit the gym hard or worked a job that required manual labor, because he didn't carry an ounce of flab.

When they were almost done with the meal, Harrison Holmes stood and addressed the entire clan.

"The luggage won't be delivered until after

the muster, which is mandatory. This is where they give us instructions on what to do in case of emergency."

"Is the ship going to sink?" a little girl with braids down to the middle of her back asked.

"No, Zoey. I promise we won't sink," Harrison said. "Your muster point should be on the front of your door key. I think we're all in Section J, except for Indina and her friend, since they were added on at the last minute."

Griffin noticed a few more curious looks being thrown his way, but, once again, those looks were accompanied by smiles. He felt a little more at ease, especially after sharing a table with Indina's aunt and uncle-in-law, who spoke with him as if they'd known him all their lives.

After the "Welcome Aboard" buffet, there was a vessel-wide call for everyone to convene at their respective muster points where they were all told what to do in the unlikely case they would have to abandon ship. They were ordered to line up according to their cabin numbers, with the tallest person in the back. Griffin stepped in behind Indina and listened intently as their designated muster captain strutted back and forth, speaking instructions into a bullhorn while two crewmembers demonstrated how to properly secure a life jacket.

"Maybe I should have brushed up on my swimming skills," Griffin muttered.

"Let's hope none of this is necessary. I just got my hair done. I don't plan on swimming at all this weekend."

"Seriously?" Griffin asked. He looked at her soft, shoulder-length hair. It was at least four different shades, mostly deep brown with streaks of warm honey and light blonde. It looked glorious against her beautiful light brown skin.

"You can't come on a cruise and not go swimming at least once," Griffin said.

"After spending nearly two hours getting this flat-ironed, I bet I can. One drop of water and my hair will curl up into the tiniest 'fro you've ever seen."

"I like it when you wear it that way."

She looked back at him, one brow arching.

"What? You think I don't pay attention to stuff like that?" He leaned forward and placed his lips against the shell of her ear. "I notice a lot more about you than you think."

He couldn't be sure, but he thought he felt a faint tremble against him.

Just then, the crewmember with the bullhorn announced that the required muster was complete, and that all luggage should be waiting in their cabins. People swarmed the elevator bank. Griffin and Indina decided to take the stairs up to the seventh deck instead of waiting for an available car.

"Any idea where the rest of your family is staying?" Griffin asked as they walked down the narrow corridor toward their cabin.

"Harrison said they're all here in the aft

section, but on the fifth floor. Because our cabin was booked at the last minute, we had to take what they had left." She tapped her keycard to the electronic pad and opened the door to their cabin. "Thankfully, all they had left was this junior suite."

The nautically decorated cabin was small by normal hotel room standards, but larger than Griffin had anticipated for a cruise ship. In addition to a queen bed, there was a separate seating area with a sofa, a small table and two chairs, and what he supposed was considered a wet bar. There was also an entertainment center, though the equipment looked a bit dated.

"We have a veranda," he said, bypassing their bags as he walked over to the sliding doors and opened them. Warm air instantly flooded the room.

"Oh, this is nice," Indina said as she joined him on the small balcony. "I can totally see myself out here enjoying a cup of coffee in the morning while doing a little dolphin watching."

"It would be cool as hell if we saw dolphins."

"I know, right? I'm starting to warm up to this cruise idea."

"Seeing as we have three days on this boat, I should hope so." Griffin laughed. He folded his arms over the balcony's thick railing and looked out at the New Orleans skyline. "This is a helluva view."

"I'll be happy when the view is of a nice

beach and clear blue water." She fanned herself. "I sure hope there's a breeze once the ship actually starts moving."

"Yeah, it's hot as hell out here," Griffin said, pushing back from the balcony railing and gesturing for Indina to lead the way back into the cabin. Once inside, he perched himself on the table and crossed his feet at the ankles. Folding his arms over his chest, Griffin asked, "So what exactly does one do on a cruise, besides consume more shrimp than any single person should eat in one sitting?"

"Those shrimps were pretty damn good." Indina laughed.

"I'm hoping they'll have more tomorrow," he said. "But other than eating, what is there to do? I've never been on a cruise before, so I have no idea."

"Neither have I," Indina said. "I know we have dinner every night at seven fifteen, and that we have a family excursion to see some Mayan ruins once we get to the Yucatan. But other than that..." She shrugged.

A thick silence filled the room, sucking the air out of it. Several uneasy moments ticked by as they both stood there in the awkward stillness.

Indina gestured to the bed. "We could always have sex."

He nodded. "Works for me."

Griffin pushed away from the table, grabbing his shirt by the collar and pulling it over his head as he made his way to the bed. He toed his shoes off and did away with his socks before unsnapping his jeans and pushing them, along with his boxers, down his hips. He helped Indina with her pants, tugging them off her legs and tossing them on the sofa. Griffin grabbed a condom from his wallet before chucking that aside as well.

He stood at the edge of the bed while Indina unhooked her bra and gently folded it.

"Is there a reason you're treating that bra as if it's breakable?"

"It was expensive. I don't want the cups to collapse," she said, placing the bra on the tiny bedside shelf. Then she sat on the edge of the bed, spread her thighs on either side of his legs and drew him toward her. "Now give me this," she said. Wrapping her palm around the base of his semi-hard cock, she pumped her hand up and down his length several times before drawing it into her mouth with one long, slow suck.

Griffin's head fell back with his groan. Nothing in this world gave him more pleasure than being surrounded by Indina's warm mouth. He closed his eyes and concentrated on the sensation of her tongue gliding along the underside of his dick. There was nothing better than this. Nothing.

He shoved his hand in her hair, gripping the back of her head as she swallowed him whole. Her gorgeous lips slid up and down his length, not stopping until he was hard as a brick. She released him with a loud pop, then tore opened the condom packet and rolled the latex over his erection.

"That's better," she said as she pushed back onto the bed and spread her legs wide for him.

Griffin didn't know if he wanted to start with his mouth or his cock, but Indina made the decision for him. She grabbed his shoulders and pulled him down on top of her. He wedged himself between her thighs, hooked his arm under her knee and placed her right leg over his shoulder. He'd learned from much experience that it was her favorite position.

Gripping his erection in his hand, he guided it inside her moist heat.

Their matching moans of pleasure bounced off the cabin's thin walls. It didn't matter how many times they did this, he would never get over the initial sensation of her snug body surrounding his hardness. It obliterated every other thought in his head. Once he connected with Indina in this most intimate way, it was all he could think about.

Griffin eased nearly all the way out before driving his hips forward. He braced his hands on either side of her and dipped his head, wrapping his lips around her rigid nipple and sucking gently. He knew the suction drove her wild, and right now driving her wild was at the very top of his agenda. She held his head to her breast and dug her heel into his back, her pelvis lifting to meet his thrusts.

"My God, Griffin," she shouted.

He lifted his head and grinned. "It's a good thing your family is on a different floor. I'm sure the entire deck just heard you."

She burst out laughing, but it turned into another moan as he once again buried himself deep inside her wet heat. He rolled his hips, his knees digging into the hard, unfamiliar mattress.

He peered down at Indina and nearly lost his mind at the look of sheer bliss on her face.

God, he wanted to kiss her. He ached to dip his head and snag her plump bottom lip between his teeth. He wanted to thrust his tongue inside her mouth to the same rhythm he was thrusting his cock inside her body.

But that just wasn't how they operated. She'd willingly shared her body with him, but her kiss? He had yet to fully taste it.

Griffin blocked those thoughts out of his mind and focused on what he was feeling. That's what mattered right now. The feeling of Indina tight and wet around him. Feeling her walls caress him as he slid deep. He pumped his hips and clasped his lips over her protruding nipple again, swirling his tongue around the tight bud before nipping at it with his teeth.

Indina's breathy mewls of pleasure drizzled down his spine, fueling the pleasure that coursed along his skin.

He was close. So damn close. *Too* damn close.

He wanted to make this last longer. Make her come over and over again. But that wasn't going to happen this time.

Despite his best effort to stave off his impending orgasm, Griffin knew he was only moments from losing it. He snuck a hand between them and zeroed in on her clit, rubbing his fingers over the slippery bundle of nerves until he felt Indina's inner walls constricting around his cock. The pressure building at the base of his spine exploded and his entire body quaked with the ferocity of the orgasm that rushed through him.

Indina's back bowed off the bed as she came with him, her limbs trembling, her head rolling back as she screamed at the ceiling.

Griffin rolled off her and collapsed onto his back, his heart pounding in time with the thumping music coming from several decks above them. Even louder were his and Indina's heavy pants echoing off the cabin walls.

"How can you be so damn good at that?" Indina said between breaths.

"I used to sneak peeks at my mom's old paperback romance novels," he answered. "Best manual a teenage boy could ask for."

Indina looked over at him and burst out laughing, then she looked back up at the ceiling and released a satisfied sigh.

After a couple of quiet minutes passed, Griffin asked, "Now what do we do?"

"I don't know," she said. "This is usually

when I get dressed and go home."

Neither of them spoke as that hard truth settled in. Unless they were at work or having sex, there wasn't much else they did together.

"This is going to be awkward, isn't it?" Indina asked.

"Probably." *Definitely*.

She looked over at him. "When I invited you along, I didn't really think about all the time we'd have to spend together *not* doing what we normally do when we're together."

Griffin levered himself up on his elbow. "I'm okay spending all our time having sex if you're up for it."

She laughed again, then stopped. She sat up. "Is the boat moving?"

Griffin paused. "I think so."

They both rose from the bed. Indina grabbed one of the robes hanging in the cabin's closet, and went out onto the veranda.

"I'll be out there in a minute," Griffin said.

He went into the bathroom to get rid of the condom and clean himself off, and nearly had a panic attack at how tiny the space was. *Shit*. His claustrophobic side would have a helluva time getting used to this. He threw on a pair of sweatpants and T-shirt before joining Indina on the veranda.

The boat had indeed started a slow journey down the Mississippi, the buildings of downtown New Orleans already behind them.

"How cool is this," Indina said. She'd settled

on one of the deck chairs. "I've never seen the city from this vantage point before. It really is a gorgeous town, isn't it?"

"One of the most beautiful I've ever seen," Griffin said in agreement. He pointed to the eight-story building just beyond the levee in the city's Bywater neighborhood. "That was the first building I worked on after moving to New Orleans," he said. "I thought about buying one of the condos, but I'm happy I passed. I rather like my house."

"I love your house," Indina said.

Griffin's brows rose. "I'm surprised you've noticed it. You're never there long enough to really take it all in."

She stared at him. "I know," she said softly.

"Yeah, I know too," he said.

The awkwardness took center stage once again. They'd never established an official set of rules when it came to this coworkers with benefits relationship, but there were unwritten ones that had developed over the past eight months. Like no kissing. And no acknowledgment of anything other than a working relationship once they were beyond the walls of his bedroom.

That's why it had shocked the hell out of Griffin when she'd asked him to join her on this cruise. It had given him a small shred of hope that he could maybe convince her to move beyond their weekly hookups and try to start up something more serious.

"So, what else should we do?" Indina asked. "We've already agreed that we can't have sex the entire weekend."

"Did we come to an agreement on that?"

"Yes." Her throaty laugh pulled at his groin. "My body needs recovery time." She stretched her legs out in front of her. "The only other thing we do together is work, and we are *not* doing that while we're on this ship." Her eyes narrowed. "You didn't bring your laptop, did you?"

Griffin shook his head. "It's been about three years since I had a bona fide vacation. I want to enjoy myself this weekend."

"Good. We deserve it after all the work we put into that last project."

Indina stood and stretched her arms over her head, then she folded them on the veranda's railing and stared out at the levee.

"I probably should have Googled 'What to do on a cruise' before I agreed to take one," she said.

"The only thing I know about cruises is what I've seen on the occasional episode of *The Love Boat* on *Nick at Nite*."

She looked back over her shoulder. "You watch Nickelodeon?"

"Sometimes," he admitted with a grin.

She turned, resting her elbows on the railing. Her robe gaped just a little, revealing the shadow between her thighs. Suddenly, the thought of going for another round in bed was the only thing he could think about. The appendage between his legs was more than ready for it.

"What did they do on *The Love Boat*? Other than love stuff?" Indina asked.

"Shuffleboard."

That smile broke out across her face again. "Okay, then. I say we go play ourselves some shuffleboard."

Indina slumped against the cue stick as she waited for Griffin to take his turn. Thankfully she still had cell service because she'd had to search the Web for the rules of shuffleboard when they arrived on the fourth deck and discovered that neither of them knew how to play. She was still confused as to exactly how — or more accurately *why*—someone would want to play this game, but she'd dragged Griffin out here so she felt obligated to play. If he wanted to live out his *Love Boat* dreams then she would continue with this stupid game.

Griffin shoved the disk into the number eight triangle. "Your turn," he said.

Indina stifled her sigh behind a tight smile and returned to the base of the shuffleboard court. She sent the cue stick forward, but stopped moments before hitting the disk. She looked over at Griffin and said, "I'm sorry, but I can't take much more of this. It's boring as hell."

He dropped his head back and let out an exasperated breath. "Thank God you finally said something. I was just thinking that I'd rather throw myself overboard than spend another five minutes doing this."

Indina burst out laughing. "Why didn't you say anything?"

"I thought you wanted to play." Taking the cue stick from her hand, he set them both back into the racks hanging on the wall.

"What do you say we both make sure the other actually *wants* to do something before making assumptions?" Indina asked. "We're only on this ship for three days. That's a half hour of our time we will never get back."

"Agreed," Griffin said with a nod. "What about a tour of the ship? Does the thought of that make you want to bang your head against the wall?"

She tilted her head to the side. "I'd like that. As big as this ship is, there has to be something more entertaining than shuffleboard to keep us occupied."

Griffin leaned forward and whispered into her ear in a silky, seductive voice. "When it comes to keeping occupied, I prefer my original suggestion."

Desire flooded Indina's bloodstream. She was starting to rethink his suggestion, as well. Would it really be a bad thing to spend the next three days naked in bed with this man? If it weren't for the fact that her entire nosy ass family was on this ship, Indina would consider doing exactly that.

"I promise we'll have plenty of time to make good on your suggestion," she said.

She was struck by the intensity in his gaze as he dipped his head and looked her directly in the eyes. "I'm holding you to that," Griffin said.

The sliding door nearest to them opened and her cousins, Elijah and Tobias, along with their wives, Monica and Sienna, walked out. Indina had already figured she would run into a Holmes or two around every corner this weekend. The ship was massive, but so was the Holmes clan.

"Well, hello there," Monica said, her eyes crinkling at the corners. The emergency room doctor had won over their entire family when she moved to New Orleans and turned Indina's freewheeling bachelor cousin into the quintessential family man. Monica had also turned into a bit of a matchmaker. Last year she'd tried to set Indina up with two doctors and a hospital administrator. All three dates were disastrous.

"I'm Monica." She stuck her hand out to Griffin. "A Holmes by marriage, as is my sister-in-law, Sienna. This is Eli and Toby."

"My cousins," Indina interjected. "What are you guys up to?"

"We're going on a behind-the-scenes tour of the galley," Sienna said. She looked radiant, despite her seven months pregnant belly. Or maybe it was because of it. "There's a promise of dessert samples."

"You can eat after that huge buffet we just had?" Indina asked.

"You think I can't?" Sienna said, rubbing her plump belly.

"Believe me, she can," Toby said, earning an elbow to the gut from his wife.

"I'd invite you both to join us, but you had to book the tour in advance," Monica said. "Sorry."

Indina waved off her apology. "Don't worry about us. We're going to take a self-guided tour. We'll see you all at dinner tonight. That is, if you aren't too stuffed from your galley tour."

"We won't be," Sienna called over her shoulder.

"It was nice to officially meet you," Monica said to Griffin. "I look forward to chatting later."

"Enjoy your tour," Indina said, stepping between them. She could see those matchmaker wheels turning behind Monica's eyes.

As she and Griffin entered the corridor, he asked, "Exactly how many people are in your family?"

Indina chuckled. "Too many. I know it's pretty overwhelming. But when I think about it, our family is small compared to most families in New Orleans. My dad and my late uncle Wesley were my grandparents' only children. Uncle Wesley and Margo had three sons — Alex, Eli and Toby. My mom and dad had four kids."

"So I still have a brother to meet," Griffin stated.

She nodded. "Ezra was the tall one with the wire-rimmed glasses. You'll get to meet him eventually."

"They're all the size of oak trees," Griffin said.

"That seems to be a trait of the Holmes men," Indina said.

"And you're the only girl," he said. "Where do you fit in the line?"

"Harrison's the oldest, with me next. We're fourteen months apart. Mom and dad waited a few years before they had Ezra."

"What about the youngest? His name is Reid, right?"

She nodded. "Reid was the surprise of the bunch. My mom found out she was pregnant when I was twelve. It was so embarrassing."

Griffin chuckled. "Why is that?"

"Because I was in the seventh grade, and by that time we all knew how babies were made. Knowing what my parents had to do in order to make a baby grossed me out." Indina did an exaggerated shudder, and Griffin laughed harder.

"I guess that's enough to scar any kid."

"Totally and completely," Indina said. "It took months before I could look either of them in the eye."

Indina stopped to look at a cute bathing suit in the window of one of the gift shops aboard the ship.

"So, where's your mom?" Griffin asked. "I just realize I haven't met her yet."

Indina looked over at him and frowned. "She died earlier this year."

His head jerked back in surprise. "This year? When?"

"Early March," Indina answered.

A blanket of astonishment still covering his face, Griffin backed into an alcove that held several purple, velvet-covered chairs.

"How did I not know you lost your mother?" he asked as he took a seat.

That was a good question. "I guess the topic never came up," Indina said, settling into the chair next to his.

It was suddenly painful for her to swallow. It didn't have as much to do with talking about her mother's death as it did with the bewildering question swirling around in her head. How could she be intimate with someone for as long as she and Griffin had been, yet not share such a crucial detail of her life?

Granted, her mother died only a few months after she and Griffin started sleeping together, but it was startling to realize a man she'd shared her body with countless times didn't even know that she'd suffered the single most significant loss of her life earlier this year. How *had* this topic never come up?

But, then again, why would it? When it came to their personal lives, they never shared all that much. She had no idea if his parents were dead or alive. The thought left an uncomfortable knot lodged in Indina's throat. She knew more about her mailman's background than she did about Griffin's.

"I'm sorry about your mom." Griffin took her left hand in his and caressed her palm with his thumb. "How did she die?"

"Heart disease," Indina answered.

"The silent killer."

She nodded. "That's exactly what it is. My mom walked three miles every morning, tried to eat as healthy as one can while living in New Orleans, and took her blood pressure medication religiously. Yet it still got her." Indina shook her head. "So many people don't realize that heart disease is the number one killer of black women. My brothers and I have been trying to figure out what we can do to raise awareness in my mom's name. We're leaning toward setting up a foundation with a goal of educating more women about their risks."

"That would be a beautiful legacy," he said.

"Thank you," Indina replied. She'd come to terms with her mother's death but sometimes, when she least expected it, it hit her that she was gone. The pain could be overwhelming.

"So, was it rough growing up the only girl in the family?" Griffin asked, as if he sensed that she wanted to change the subject.

Indina gratefully latched on to the new topic. "Not at all." She looked over at him and grinned. "I was spoiled rotten. When I said I never got whippings, it wasn't because I didn't deserve any. I definitely deserved a few. But my dad never once gave me so much as a swat on the butt. It used to drive my brothers nuts because they never got off that easy. I'm lucky they still don't hold it against me."

"It seems as if you all get along okay," he said.

"The entire Holmes family is close-knit. Honestly, I don't know why they're even calling this a reunion at all. It's not as if we all don't see each other on a regular basis. We're together for every holiday, and if there's too much time between holidays, someone will throw a picnic in their backyard for no reason other than getting the family together."

"Sounds pretty great to me," Griffin said. There was a note of longing in his voice. She'd go so far as to call it envy. It sparked Indina's curiosity.

"What about your family?" she asked.

He shrugged. "Much smaller than yours. It's just me, my parents and my older brother. They're all still in Milwaukee."

"Any extended family?"

"Yeah, but they're mostly scattered around the country. I haven't seen my cousins in years."

Indina frowned. It occurred to her that in the year she'd known him, Griffin had never visited his family or, as far as she knew, had them down to visit him. An entire year without seeing his family?

So much of her time—outside of the hours she spent at work and hanging out with a few close friends—was cannibalized by one Holmes gathering after another, but Indina couldn't imagine life any other way. As much as she complained about her family's clinginess, she would hate it if she didn't get to see them on a regular basis. Hearing Griffin talk about his made her appreciate her rambunctious, sometimes annoying, often too nosy clan.

She and Griffin continued down the cruise ship's broad main corridor, with its floors that were so polished they looked wet, and its dozens of shops. There was a high-end boutique with formalwear for the cruise's dress-up night, several souvenir gift shops, even a coffee bar and a salon. The most crowded room looked to be the duty-free liquor store.

"You can live on this cruise ship if you wanted to," Griffin said. "They have everything."

"I hear that's becoming a thing."

"Living on a cruise ship?"

She nodded. "Especially for retirees. Just think about it. You don't have to worry about cooking or cleaning, and you get to travel the world. Sounds like a pretty sweet life to me."

Amusement brightened his deep brown eyes. "Not sure I can handle being on the water that long, but I can be persuaded," he said with a wink.

Okay, exactly what was going on here? This wasn't the first time he'd hit her with that sexy wink, but for some reason it spawned a new, unfamiliar flutter in her belly.

Indina pushed the odd feeling out of her head with the promise to revisit it later, when she had time to unpack and fully examine the inexplicable awareness Griffin's single wink had elicited.

She pointed to the sliding doors leading to the outside deck. "I think there's a stairway that leads to the upper deck," she said.

They went outside and walked up a set of wooden stairs. It brought them directly to one of the pools where they encountered another gaggle of Holmeses. All of the kids were there, along with Harrison and Alexander. Indina made introductions.

"Alex here is my grandparents' eldest grandchild," Indina said. "He's the reason Eli and Toby both had such a hard time living up to their big brother's example."

"They did okay," Alex said, reaching over to shake Griffin's hand.

She tried pointing out the kids in the pool, but gave up.

"You'll meet them eventually," she said. "And then promptly forget their names because there's just too many of them these days." She turned to her brother. "Have you seen Ezra? I need to talk to him."

"Last I heard, he and Reid were going down

to the concierge to book a Jet Ski excursion for our afternoon in Progresso."

"I thought we were all going out to see the Mayan ruins?"

"We are, but they went down to see if there's a way for them to fit in the Jet Skis on the same day." Harrison shook his head. "They won't be able to, but I'll let the people at the excursion desk break it to them. Knowing those two, they'll waste their money on the second excursion anyway."

Griffin turned to her. "I didn't realize the excursions were extra. Who do I pay for that?"

"It's included with the price of the cruise," Indina said.

"No, it isn't," Harrison said. Indina turned to him and gave him an annoyed look. "What?" her brother asked.

She turned her attention back to Griffin. "Don't worry about the excursion. I've got you covered."

"Wait a minute—" Griffin started, but Alex cut him off.

Clamping a hand on Griffin's back, he said, "I don't even know you, but you're already my hero. You've acquired what many a man could only hope to find: a sugar mama."

"Oh, shut up," Indina said with a laugh. "It's not like that. I invited Griffin to come along. He shouldn't have to pay for anything."

"But I will," Griffin said. He turned to Harrison, as if her brother was the one he was most afraid of offending. "I'm paying my own way."

Harrison held his hands up. "It's not my business."

Indina rolled her eyes. "We'll catch up with you all later," she said. "We still have to visit the forward and midship areas of this deck."

"Check out the ice cream shop," Alex called.

As soon as they stepped away from the pool area, Griffin turned to her.

"Okay, that wasn't cool," he said.

"What?"

"First of all, you're not paying for my cruise. Let's establish that right here and right now." Indina folded her arms across her chest but remained silent. "Secondly, why would you even say those things in front of your brother and cousin? They probably think I'm some kind of mooch living off of you or something."

She shrugged. "They think I'm your sugar mama. Alex is impressed, and it takes a lot to impressed that one."

"Indina—"

"Come on," she said, capturing his wrist and tugging. "We still have a lot of boat to see."

A few minutes later they reached a quiet sundeck in the middle of the ship. The serene atmosphere was the polar opposite of the mayhem on the lido deck and main pool area.

"Now *this* is how you relax," she said, pointing to a couple of plush lounge chairs. "Finding the time to sit out here with my book just became my number one priority."

"Can we finish the conversation we were just having?" Griffin asked.

"And what conversation was that?"

"The one where we assure your family that I'm not a gold digger taking advantage of their sweet little Indina?"

She stared at him for a moment before she burst out laughing, interrupting the peacefulness surrounding them. She laughed until she felt a pinch in her side. Then she looked up at Griffin's deadpan expression and laughed even harder.

Once she was finally able to catch her breath, she wiped tears of mirth from her eyes and held up both hands.

"Let me assure you that *no one* in my family would ever think that. They know that sweet little Indina can take care of herself." She swiped again at the moisture on her cheeks. "Look, if you want to pay for your excursion, that's fine, but I *am* paying for your cruise. I would have had to pay for the cabin whether you were here or not."

Griffin stuck his hands in his pockets and tipped his head to the side. His dark brown eyes crinkled at the corners with the wry grin that curved at the edges of his lips.

"You seem amused," Indina said. "Don't keep it all to yourself. What's so funny?"

"I just realized that there hasn't been an occasion this past year where you had the chance to see just how stubborn I am."

Her brows arched. "Oh, so you think you can out stubborn me?"

"Over this? No doubt." Griffin leaned forward. "When it comes to a battle of wills, I always win, Indina. Always."

Indina couldn't stop the smile from traveling across her lips. "We'll see about that."

Chapter Three

By the time he and Indina arrived at dinner, nearly all of the seats were taken at the three tables the Holmes family occupied on the far left side of the massive dining room. There were two open spots next to her aunt Margo, but Indina walked past that table, instead going to where her brothers sat, along with Eli and Monica.

Damn. So much for a nice, relaxing dinner. He would have much preferred engaging in easy conversation with her aunt. Being stuck at a table with her intimidating as hell brothers, he was guaranteed to be on edge the entire time.

Griffin pulled out Indina's chair, and then took the one next to the window, which afforded a view of the inky black night. A thumbnail slice of moon provided the only glimmer of light as it cut across the water.

"So, what were you two doing to have you showing up so late?" Monica asked. Indina told him earlier that Monica was an ER doctor at the same hospital where Eli served as the head of obstetrics.

"Napping," Indina answered her.

"Napping?" Monica's brows arched. "Is that what they're calling it these days?"

Harrison Holmes cleared his throat. "For the

record, I don't want to hear about anything you two were doing, napping or otherwise."

"You're damn right about that," said the brother Griffin had yet to officially meet.

"Don't start," Indina said. She turned to Harrison. "Where's Willow?"

"She decided to skip dinner," he answered. "Said she had a headache."

Indina turned to Griffin. "Willow is my sister-in-law. I'll always be indebted to her for marrying this one and bringing a little more estrogen into the family. I'll introduce you to her tomorrow."

"So, I'm not worth an introduction?" Indina's middle brother asked as he rose slightly out of his chair and stuck a hand out at Griffin. "I'm Ezra."

"Griffin Sims," he answered. "Nice to meet you."

"You too. I heard you're her…uh…coworker, is it?" he asked, tipping his head toward his sister. The smirk on his lips indicated that he'd heard more than that. Apparently, that sugar mama rumor was making the rounds. Griffin would be damned if he let them all continue to think he was mooching off of Indina.

"I'm one of the head structural engineers at a top engineering firm downtown. We take on mostly large city and state government projects," Griffin explained. "Extremely large and lucrative contracts."

He was prepared to show them his damn bank balance if that's what it took to convince the men in her family that he could pay for both his and Indina's cruises.

"I wonder if we've worked on any," her youngest brother, Reid, asked. "Holmes Construction just bid on several city projects."

Griffin glanced around the table. "Wait a minute. Is the guy who owns Holmes Construction a relative?"

"He's the one who thinks I'm your sugar mama," Indina said.

Reid nodded toward the other table. "Alex owns Holmes Construction. I'm the lead plumber and sometime general foreman, depending on the size of the project."

"You guys did the renovations on the Sewage and Water Board building. That was some nice work." Griffin looked over at Indina. "How come you never mentioned you were related to those Holmeses."

"I'm related to those Holmeses," she said, her smile cheeky as hell.

He could only laugh at her flippant response. He could have guessed that she had this sassy side, but he rarely got to see it. Indina was the consummate professional during work hours, and outside of work they were usually otherwise occupied. He liked this side of her.

Hell, he liked *every* side of her. Except for the side that couldn't seem to see them as nothing more than coworkers with benefits.

Reid, who sat next to Indina, reached over his sister and stuck his hand out to Griffin. "Well, I'm happy to have you around," he said. "Especially after running into Timothy and his—hey! What the hell? Why'd you kick me, man?"

Ezra Holmes stared at his brother from across the table with downright murder in his eyes.

"What were you saying?" Indina asked Reid, even though her gaze remained on Ezra.

"He wasn't saying anything," Ezra said.

The rest of the table had become eerily quiet.

It took Griffin less than five seconds to put these puzzle pieces together. This Timothy person Reid had run into had a connection to Indina—probably an ex-boyfriend—which shot Griffin's curiosity to skyscraper levels. He knew as much about Indina's exes as she knew about his, which was hardly anything. He wanted to know whatever he could about the kind of guy she regarded worthy of the title *significant other*.

"Just spit it out," Indina said. "You ran into Timothy and...?"

"And his fiancée," Ezra said.

"Is that all?" she asked with a nonchalant wave. "Do you think I care that Timothy is getting married?"

"No, I don't," Reid said. "But apparently that one over there thinks you can't handle it."

"I never said she couldn't handle it," Ezra retorted.

"So why in the hell did you kick me under

the table?"

"Can we please move on to another subject?" Monica asked.

"Please," her husband chimed in.

Harrison, who had remained quiet throughout the exchange, signaled the table attendant for another beer.

The head table attendant introduced himself and welcomed the family to the cruise ship. As he presented his team of servers who would be attending to the needs of the entire party for the duration of the cruise, Griffin studied Indina's profile, searching for any sign that talk of her ex-boyfriend had affected her more than she was letting on. He saw none. Maybe she really didn't care that her ex was getting married.

Griffin considered how he would feel if he found out his ex-wife was engaged. He would offer to help pay for the damn wedding.

The attendant gave a rundown of tonight's menu. When Reid learned that he wasn't limited in what he could order, he proceeded to order one of every appetizer on the menu.

"What?" Reid asked as the rest of the people at the table stared at him. "I went up on the top deck and played some basketball this afternoon. I worked up an appetite."

"As if you wouldn't have ordered the same thing even if you'd been 'napping' like those two," Monica said, pointing to Indina and Griffin.

Griffin cleared his throat. Indina was a

grown woman, but that didn't mean he was comfortable with innuendoes about them sleeping together being bandied about at the dinner table, especially with her three extremely large brothers listening to every word.

Thankfully, the conversation switched to the stage show several of them had watched in the huge theater right before dinner. Within minutes, an army of servers showed up with their appetizers and everyone settled in for the meal.

As they ate, Indina pointed out the people Griffin hadn't met yet. Her niece and nephew, fifteen-year-old Liliana and eight-year-old Athens, sat at the table with Eli and Monica's twins, Finnegan and Fawn, and Alex Holmes's kids, Sebastian and Jasmine. There wasn't a chance in hell that he could ever remember all the names she rattled off.

During the salad course, Alex's wife, Renee, moved over to the kids' table, because Sebastian wouldn't stop fighting with his older sister. Their squabble reminded Griffin of how his own niece and nephew would fight at the dinner table. It brought on a smile that was swiftly replaced by a frown. A heavy ache settled in his gut.

Being here in the midst of the Holmeses, seeing how well they all got along—despite Indina's good-natured bickering with her brothers—was a stark reminder of just how much he missed spending time with his own family. Griffin knew it would only take a phone call. A simple call and he could have this again. He could sit across the table from his only sibling. He could enjoy learning about what was going on in his niece and nephew, Desiree and Garland, Jr's, lives. If only he could bring himself to make that one simple phone call.

But it wasn't *making* the phone call that was stopping him. It's what he'd have to say once his brother picked up the other line.

I'm sorry.

You were right.

I was wrong.

Yeah, that wasn't happening anytime soon.

He would have to be content with hanging out on the fringes of Indina's family, soaking in as much of this special bonding time as possible. Maybe he *was* a mooch. He was mooching off her family's closeness.

He quietly observed them as they progressed through the rest of the meal, until her brother, Ezra, brought Griffin into a discussion about New Orleans's local sports team, trying to get him to break up a tie. Half of the table thought the local NBA franchise would be the next one to bring a national championship to the city, while the others at the table banked on it being the Saints.

"Well, being a football fan, I'd have to go with the Saints," Griffin said.

Ezra shook his head. "I thought maybe we could be friends, but I see that shit won't happen." Then he grinned. "I'm just messing with you."

"Speaking of friends." Indina looked over at Ezra. "I have a message to you from Mackenna. Leave her alone."

"Mackenna Arnold?" Harrison asked. "Where's she been? I haven't seen her in a while."

"Except when she's on the news going toe-to-toe with a reporter about some decision the city council has made," Eli said.

"Yeah, well these days she's being hounded by a certain journalist," Indina said, staring pointedly at her brother.

Ezra held up his hands. "I'm just doing my job."

"You're being a pain in the ass. I don't know what kind of juicy story you think you're going to find, but you're looking in the wrong place. Mack is one of the most honest people I know."

"She's a politician," Ezra replied, as if that said it all.

"I mean it, Ezra. Knock it off."

Her brother looked at Indina over his wineglass, but didn't comment further.

Griffin would have never pegged him as a journalist. He looked as if he belonged on a construction site with Alex and Reid, or laying guys out on a football field, instead of working behind a desk.

After scraping up the last of the sauce from his plate of duck a l'orange, Griffin set his fork down and took a deep breath. "Now I see why people choose to live on a cruise ship. If this is the way you get to eat every night, why would you ever want to cook for yourself again?"

"Tell me about it," Indina said. "I already decided that I can eat nothing but kale and air next week."

"Just get in a little exercise. You'll be fine."

Her right brow lifted in the sexiest arch. In a slightly lowered voice, she said, "You do realize my main workouts involve you, right? You think you can handle more?"

Holy. Shit.

Griffin had to take another sizable breath after that one. And now all he could think about was his and Indina's own brand of working out.

The waiter had just taken their desserts when a tall guy who looked vaguely familiar walked up to the table with a gorgeous, honey-toned beauty tucked to his side.

"Evening everyone. Sorry we're a little late," the guy said.

"A *little* late? Try an hour," Toby called from the other table.

"Sorry about that. We were busy," the guy said.

"I guess they were 'napping' too," Monica said with a snort.

Indina leaned over and whispered in Griffin's ear, "That's Jonathan Campbell. A friend of the family."

The name instantly registered. Jonathan

owned a high-end sports bar in the city.

"I'm not sure who the woman is," she continued. "His newest flavor of the month, I guess."

He heard the hint of disgust in her tone. "I'm guessing you don't approve?"

Indina shrugged. "I was rooting for someone else. It's a long story."

Jonathan came over to where they were sitting and placed a kiss on Indina's cheek. "Been a long time since I've seen you," he told her. He stuck a hand out to Griffin, introducing himself.

"Nice to meet you," Griffin said. "I've been to your sports bar a few times. It's one of my favorite spots in the city."

"I appreciate it," he said. "You can thank this lady right here for the decor."

He turned to Indina. "You decorated The Hard Court?"

She nodded. "It was my first foray into something other than residential interior design."

"Speaking of nightclubs, I hear the adults are planning to hit the club here on the ship," Harrison said.

"Except for the pregnant adult, who is planning to hit the sheets," Sienna called from the table next to theirs.

"Well, there's free babysitting until one a.m. on this boat, so I'm definitely hitting the club," Monica said. "I can count on one hand the number of times Eli and I have had a night out dancing since the twins were born."

Indina looked over at him. "What do you say? You up for some dancing?"

Griffin hesitated. "I'm not much of a dancer."

"Neither am I, but this is supposed to be vacation, remember?"

He grinned. "Don't say I didn't warn you."

The ship's onboard discotheque was as cheesy and outdated as one would expect a discotheque aboard a cruise ship to be, but for Indina it only added to the charm. Just as the first bars of the Bee Gees's "Stayin' Alive" began, several spotlights zeroed in on the gaudy disco ball above the dance floor. Members of the cruise's entertainment crew came out of a side door, all dressed in 1970s garb. They congregated underneath the glittery ball and struck the John Travolta pose from *Saturday Night Fever*.

The crowd went wild.

The dancers broke apart and came for the crowd, encouraging passengers to join them. When one of the crewmembers dragged Ezra to the middle of the dance floor and started doing The Bump, Indina laughed so hard her knees started to buckle. She and Monica had to hold each other up to prevent themselves from collapsing. Her poor brother looked like an injured crane as he tried to keep up with the dancer, who didn't fare much better.

She laughed even harder when Griffin became the dancer's next victim. He was so bad he made Ezra look like a top contender on *Dancing With The Stars*.

"I can't...take this," Indina said. "Every...time I try...to catch my breath...I start laughing again."

"I'm gonna piss my pants," Monica said, which set off even more laughs.

By the time Griffin managed to free himself from the dancer, Indina could barely stand. She held onto her side.

"When you said you weren't much of a dancer, I thought you meant you just didn't *like* to dance, not that you don't know *how* to dance. That was painful."

"Hey, at least I tried," he said. "I don't see you out there."

Indina took a step back and sized him up. "Is that a challenge?"

He looked her up and down. "Either you get out there and shake that fine ass, or admit that you don't know how to dance either."

"Oh, it's on." She grabbed him by the wrist and dragged him back onto the dance floor as the deejay started a string of KC and The Sunshine Band hits. By the time "That's the Way I Like It" ended, Indina thought she would pass out from exhaustion.

Just as she was about to suggest taking a breather, the crowd formed a Soul Train line. Monica and Eli went first, dancing to Chic's "Le Freak." She and Griffin were up next. Indina knew she looked like a fool, but she didn't care. It had been so damn long since she'd had this kind of fun. The entire Holmes clan seemed to be having a good time, with the exception of Harrison, who sat with his elbows on the bar and a blank expression on his face.

The flicker of unease she'd felt at dinner over Harrison's cool dismissal of Willow's headache returned. Indina wasn't sure what to make of it.

The disco's theme segued from '70's to '80's music — the music of her childhood. She jammed to The Gap Band, DeBarge and Teena Marie. The deejay played a stretch of Michael Jackson hits, and the room went wild yet again. Indina was convinced the boat's rocking was no longer due to the waves, but to all the people on the dance floor.

"Oh, my God," Indina said as she and Griffin finally made their way to one of the tables. "I don't have to worry about counting calories anymore. I just burned enough of them to eat whatever I want for the rest of this cruise."

He put his lips to her ear. "But we can still work out later tonight, right?"

His seductively whispered words went straight to her nipples.

"Definitely," she answered. "You ready to

go right now?"

The grin that stretched across his handsome face was much too sexy. "You don't think it's too early to turn in?"

Indina didn't answer. Instead, she grabbed him by the wrist again and tugged.

"It's not even nine thirty yet," Griffin said once they entered the hallway.

"I didn't say I was ready to head back to the room, but my bones can't take any more dancing. I can already tell that my knees will hurt like a bitch tomorrow."

Griffin chuckled. "You sound like you're eighty years old."

"I was a runner for a long time. It's hard on the knees."

His head reared back slightly. "Really? I didn't know you were a runner."

She nodded. "I've been running for years, but I started cutting back after my twentieth marathon. Like I said, too hard on the knees. These days I stop after about five miles."

As they approached the midship elevators, Griffin continued to stare at her, an astonished expression blanketing his face.

"What?" Indina asked.

"After all this time, how am I just discovering that you and I have this in common?"

"You run too?"

"I've finished in the top five hundred of the Crescent City Classic for the last three years in a row."

"You run the CCC?"

He nodded. "I've participated every single year since I moved to New Orleans."

And she'd participated since she finished college. Very few things induced more pride than her collection of T-shirts from the Crescent City Classic races she'd run over the years. Funny that they'd both participated in the same race, yet had no idea that the other enjoyed the sport.

"So, the top five hundred, huh?" Indina asked as she boarded the elevator. "That's pretty impressive, especially when there's at least twenty thousand runners who take part every year. That means you must run, what, a seven-minute mile?"

"Six and a half, if I train properly and lay off the potato chips."

Her brows rose. "Impressive indeed. Maybe we should go running together sometime."

The minute the words left her mouth, Indina wanted to snatch them back.

No. No. *No!*

Invitations to go running together didn't fit into this thing she had going with Griffin. There was no room for shared interests outside of work and his bed. It tiptoed too close to the edge of a relationship. She was *not* going there again. She was done with those battle scars.

Maybe you should have thought about that before inviting him on this cruise.

It was far too late for recriminations over the cruise invite, but just because they were on this ship together, it didn't mean they were spiraling headfirst into relationship territory. She still had time to bring this thing back to friendly coworkers who just so happened to hook up on a regular basis.

"We should finish our tour," Indina said as the elevator dinged their arrival on the fourth deck. "I haven't seen the bow of the ship yet. I want to recreate my favorite scene from Titanic." She spread her arms out as if she were getting ready to fly.

"You're not balancing on the front of the ship," Griffin said.

"Don't spoil my fun," Indina said with a laugh. But when they arrived at the bow, she discovered there was no way to get to the ship's pointy front.

"Guess I won't be recreating my favorite scene."

"Thank God," Griffin said after releasing an exaggerated sigh of relief.

Indina stuck her tongue out at him like a petulant child, wrenching out a laugh from him. He backed up against the polished wood railing and crossed his arms over his chest.

"So, what are some of your other favorites?" he asked.

She tilted her head to the side in question.

Griffin shrugged. "It occurred to me tonight that I don't really know much about you outside of work."

Which is exactly the way she wanted it. Her unease must have shown on her face, because he put his hands up and said, "I'm not asking you to pour out all your deepest, darkest secrets. Just share a little...stuff."

"What kind of stuff? What is there to know?"

"Well, I didn't know that you like to dance, or that you have such bad taste in movies."

Indina gasped. "I do not."

"Titanic? I've tried to watch that twice. Fell asleep both times."

"That means *you're* the one with bad taste in movies."

"Don't worry, I won't hold it against you," he said with a devilish grin that made her stomach flip in extremely interesting ways.

Shit. She did *not* want this. Stomach flips and those little flutters she'd experienced several times today were not a part of the deal. She needed things to return to how they were before they'd boarded this ship.

What she had going with Griffin was safe. She could detach her head and her heart from it and just focus on the mutual pleasure they brought to each other. Emotion played no part in it.

But how could she stand here and ignore his request, especially after he'd joined her on this cruise at the last minute? It wasn't the ultimate sacrifice, by any means, but he still didn't have to be here. She owed it to him to play along.

"What exactly do you want to know?" Indina asked.

He folded his arms over his chest again. "I want to know if you're making other bad choices, like using Tabasco instead of Sriracha."

"I'm a Louisiana native. I only use Crystal Hot Sauce."

"See, I didn't know that."

Indina chuckled. "Really, Griffin, what's this all about?"

"I'm curious about you. Is that so hard to believe?"

"So, we've been doing this thing for eight months, yet you're all of a sudden curious about the kind of hot sauce I use?"

"It's not all of a sudden," he said. "I've been curious about you for a while. But you've never given me the chance to get to know you better. As soon as we're done in bed, you run away." He gestured to the open water. "There's nowhere for you to run now."

Indina did her best to ignore the panic that slashed through her. This was fine. There was no need to panic. Sharing a few harmless tidbits about herself didn't equate to a lifelong commitment. It wasn't as if Griffin could turn around and hurt her with anything she told him tonight.

Just play along.

"So, is this twenty questions, or what?" Indina asked him.

He shook his head. "Not twenty. I'm good with five."

She backed up against the railing and mimicked his pose. "What do you want to know?" She held up a finger. "Just so you know, we're taking turns. You ask a question, and I get to ask one."

"Fair enough. You want to go first?"

She nodded. "I'll make this first one easy. How do you like working at Sykes-Wilcox?"

"Why? Are you thinking about joining an actual firm?" he asked jokingly.

"I'm the one asking the questions, remember? And…maybe."

Indina could tell that she'd shocked him with her answer.

"I thought you enjoyed freelancing."

"I do, but my last five jobs have been with Sykes-Wilcox." She shrugged. "Why not jump on board and have them pay for my health insurance?"

"I can't argue with that. And I know Mark would love to have you on staff." He hesitated for a moment before he said, "I'm just not sure how much longer I'll be there."

It was Indina's turn to jerk back in surprise. "Really? Are you being lured away by another outfit?"

"Yeah, in a way. I'm thinking of branching out on my own." He held his hands up. "It won't happen any time soon. Probably not for another three or so years, but my plan is to save enough money so that I can take a year off, and then after that year, open up my own engineering firm."

"You're a talented engineer, Griffin. I think you would do amazingly on your own."

The gratitude in his smile warmed Indina from the inside out. "Thanks for saying that."

"What would you do with the time off?" Indina asked. She bumped him with her elbow. "Take a year-long cruise around the world?"

He chuckled. "That's tempting, but I plan to go back to Ghana."

"Back to Ghana?" She was lucky she could still stand after being hit with these back-to-back waves of shock.

Griffin nodded. "I've been there twice, but only for about a month each time. I volunteer with an organization that helps to set up filtration systems in areas without access to clean drinking water. My last trip was right before you joined the team at Sykes-Wilcox."

Indina just stared at him for several moments, completely blown away. "That's amazing, Griffin. I can't even imagine how rewarding something like that must feel."

"It's hard to describe. I've never felt more needed—as if my life were necessary—than when I was in Ghana. We take for granted how easy it is to turn on a faucet and have clean water at our fingertips. Even in those villages where we have set up the water systems, people still have to walk to the water station and carry huge jugs back to their homes. It isn't convenient by any means, but it's better than drinking water filled with parasites."

The passion in which he spoke touched something deep within Indina's soul.

"So, yeah, that's what I'm hoping to do," Griffin continued with a shrug, clearly unaware that he'd just elevated himself to superhero status in her eyes. "I want to see at least one project in Ghana through from start to finish. Once I'm done, I come back home and open up my own boutique engineering firm, one where I can control which projects I work on." He glanced over at her. "I understand that business is business, but I'm not always okay with the projects Sykes-Wilcox chooses to bid on. It's not easy when faced with working for your conscience and working to keep your job."

Several moments ticked by as Indina studied his steady features, digesting all that he'd just shared. She'd had no clue that he had this altruistic side, but then again, why would she? She'd purposely placed him in this narrow box. She'd convinced herself over these past eight months that she didn't need to know anything more about him outside of what he did while on the job or when they were naked in his bed. Anything more personal than that would put her on the slippery slope to an actual relationship. She wasn't ready for an actual relationship just yet. If ever.

No. Not if ever.

When Timothy broke things off she told herself she would not allow him to turn her into a man-hating, relationship-phobic shrew. But just the thought of investing so much of herself into something that would inevitably fall apart was too much for her to handle at the moment.

What she had going with Griffin was ideal for where she was in her life right now. Complete sexual satisfaction without messy romantic entanglements. It was perfect. Wasn't it?

"It's my turn to ask a question," Griffin said.

Indina sucked in a deep, fortifying breath. "Okay, hit me." She held her hand up. "Remember to start with an easy one."

"Okay. What's your favorite color?"

She rolled her eyes. "Not that easy."

Griffin chuckled. "But I don't know what it is."

"After all this time you don't know what my favorite color is?"

"You do realize what our relationship consists of, right? Unless your favorite color is sexy brown skin, I wouldn't have a clue."

There was no doubt her brown skin now sported a healthy dose of red. Indina had never been one to blush, but there was something about this man that had triggered the reaction way too much today.

"We've worked together enough *outside* of the bedroom for you to have picked up on my favorite color. I wear it all the time," she said.

Another shrug. "I guess I'm just not that observant. And when we're *inside* the bedroom, the only thing I'm thinking about is getting you out of your clothes."

Great. Just when she thought she had a handle on her blushing.

"It's green," Indina said. "But don't tell that to any of my sorority sisters. If I said my favorite colors were anything but crimson and cream, I'd never hear the end of it."

"You see there, I didn't know you belonged to a sorority either."

"I have the frame on my license plate. What did you think that 1913 stood for?"

He hunched his shoulder. "I had no clue."

"So I'm guessing you never pledged to a frat while in college?"

He shook his head and leaned both elbows back against the railing again. "I was too busy trying to maintain my grades so I could keep my scholarship," he admitted. "I knew my parents couldn't afford to pay tuition if I lost it, and I didn't want to be buried in student loans.

"But, if you want to know the truth, I didn't fit in with the whole Greek life. I was the nerdy kid who spent most of his time in the library or the engineering lab. I wasn't even cool enough to belong to the various engineering clubs on campus, which should tell you something right there."

She laughed. "I can't even imagine you as a geeky engineering student." She tipped her head to the side. "Actually, I could. Geeks are pretty sexy."

One brow lifted. "You think I'm sexy?"

"Do you think I'd be in your bed twice a week if I didn't?"

His deep chuckle rumbled through the air, but then his expression turned serious. "Why *are* you in my bed twice a week?"

His question, along with his suddenly earnest tone, caught her off guard. Indina shifted her weight from one foot to the other in an attempt to buy time before answering his question. She wasn't sure *how* to answer his question.

She shrugged nonchalantly. "I thought the reason was obvious. The sex is amazing."

"Look, the sex is off the charts. There's no denying that," Griffin said. "But I want to know why you've sworn off relationships."

"Who says I've sworn off relationships?"

"You did. When we first started this, you said you weren't interested in doing the 'whole relationship thing.' But you never said why."

"You never asked."

His lips tilted up in a grin. "Touché." He crossed his arms over his chest. "I'm asking now. Why have you shied away from an actual relationship?" He paused before asking, "Does it have something to do with the guy your brother mentioned at dinner?"

Indina groaned. She turned toward the water, resting her elbows on the railing as she listened to the slap of the waves breaking against the ship's hull.

Griffin's lowered voice broke through the stillness. "You don't have to talk about it if you aren't ready."

She looked at him over her shoulder. "I will never be ready to talk about Timothy with you, Griffin. That's not what this thing between us is supposed to be about." She blew out a breath. "This is exactly what I *didn't* want."

"Indina, you can trust me with this. I won't—"

She cut him off. "Please, Griffin." Taking his hand, she tugged slightly. "Can't we just go back to the cabin and do what we do best when we're together?"

His expression remained serious. When he started to pull his hand away, Indina tightened her hold.

Where was this even coming from? Goodness, she knew she shouldn't have invited him on this cruise. Without work or sex to occupy their time, she should have known he'd want to do other stuff. Like get to know her.

"Please," she pleaded. "Talking about Timothy will just put me in a horrible mood. This is supposed to be a vacation. I don't want to think about my ex on vacation."

She sensed the moment when he relented and the relief that rushed through her nearly brought her to her knees. Indina started for the door, but Griffin pulled her back. He clasped his hands on her hips and stared into her eyes.

"I won't push you to share anything you're not ready to share, but you *can* talk to me, Indina. I'm good for more than just getting you off." The barest hint of a smile reached his eyes. "But since getting you off happens to be one of my favorite pastimes, I say we go and do that right now."

Chapter Four

"Are we gonna get this game started or what?" Toby called from the left side of the beach volleyball net.

When they disembarked the ship this morning, there were three eight-seater shuttle busses waiting to escort them to an all-inclusive beach resort near the Chankanaab area of Cozumel, Mexico. Harrison had pre-booked the excursion, which included a private section of the beach for the Holmes family's exclusive use.

Indina had to give it to him. Her brother and Monica, the masterminds behind planning this cruise, had thought of everything. It was only their second day and this was already one of the best family reunions the Holmeses had ever held.

And it couldn't have come at a better time. They were inching ever closer to the six-month anniversary of her mother's passing, and Indina was worried about how her dad would handle it. Honestly, she was worried about how they all would handle it. The anniversary would fall on what would have been her mother's sixty-fifth birthday.

She watched as her dad picked eight-year-old Athens up by the waist and tossed him back into the water. The joy on his face helped to quell some of the anxiety Indina had been feeling toward him these past few months. She'd stopped asking him how he was doing after growing weary of his automatic response of "I'm fine." Clark Holmes had never been one to show his emotions. Indina just prayed that he really was dealing with her mom's death as well as he seemed to be.

It wasn't as if they hadn't known it was coming. Her mom had valiantly fought heart disease for most of her adult life, staying active and following her doctors' orders to the letter. But it hadn't been enough. She'd become weaker and weaker over these last few years, and eventually succumbed to her disease.

Indina sucked in a deep breath. The last thing her mother would want is for her to ruin this wonderful day with such melancholy thoughts.

Toby came over to the umbrella-covered beach loungers where Indina and the rest of the Holmes women had staked their claim—except for her sister-in-law, Willow, who'd taken Liliana and Jasmine to get their hair braided and buy souvenirs.

"Hey, we need a few players. Any of you want to play some volleyball?" Toby asked. He pointed to Sienna. "Not you."

Sienna dipped her head and looked at him over the rim of her sunglasses. "As if there was anything you could do to tempt me to leave this spot."

"I know one way I could tempt you," Toby said, leaning over and kissing her rounded belly. He moved to her mouth.

"Could you two wait until you have this baby before you start working on the next one," Indina said.

"Oh, honey, this is the *last* one," Sienna said.

Toby shook his head. "No, it isn't. I want a basketball team."

His wife kicked at his leg. "Get away from me."

Toby laughed as he spun the volleyball on his fingertip. "Come on, we need a couple more players. Indina? Renee? It's just until Eli and the rest of them come back from the glass-bottom boat ride."

Indina looked over at Renee. "You in?"

Renee closed the flap on her eReader cover and shoved it into her bag. "Okay. Let's do this," she said.

"Alright, alright, alright," Toby sang. "We got us some players," he called over to where Griffin, Jonathan and Reid were standing around the volleyball net.

Indina eyed Griffin as she approached. She still wasn't sure how to read him after what happened between them last night. Everything had been fine once they returned to the room and got naked. It was *after* the sex was over that things grew awkward.

Indina hadn't even come down from her

orgasmic high when the panic hit her. She realized they would have to sleep in the same bed, something they had never done before. Normally, once the sex was over, she was out the door within a matter of minutes.

Remaining in bed with Griffin had felt…weird.

But, after a while, it had also felt right. And that's what had scared her the most. She didn't want it to feel right.

The panicky feeling returned this morning when she awoke to Griffin's solid body flush against hers and his arm wrapped around her waist. She'd done her best to hide her dismay, but apprehension over how comfortable it felt to lay in his arms continued to churn in her gut.

Earlier, when they first arrived at the beach, Griffin had invited her for a walk. They'd held hands like a normal couple, and Indina had started to remember all the good parts of being in a relationship. It reminded her of how beautiful it could feel when it actually worked.

But she was still so damn gun-shy after experiencing what happened when it *didn't* work. Her heart was still too tender after being broken so badly. Not once, but twice.

It doesn't have to be that way.

Indina's chest tightened with a combination of hope and anxiety. She was mentally exhausted after fighting that voice in her head that just would not let up. For every feeble defense she attempted to erect to shield her heart, her brain countered with examples of relationships that had stood the test of time. She didn't have to look any farther than her own family. Her own parents. Her father was as committed to her mother now, even in death, as he'd been to her on their wedding day.

Was that kind of relationship still possible for her? Could she find it with Griffin?

Indina had never felt so conflicted in her life.

She stuffed those thoughts away, determined to keep her internal battle hidden from her meddling family, especially the women in her family. The one thing she did not need was her well-meaning cousins-in-law shoving her toward a relationship.

As she approached the volleyball net, Indina pasted on her brightest smile. "Ready to get schooled, boys?"

"Wait. *You're* playing?" Griffin asked.

"You sound surprised."

He hunched a shoulder. "I didn't peg you for the beach volleyball type. You seemed more at home on that lounge chair over there."

"Is that so?" Indina said. "Well, I hope you're ready to get your butt spanked."

"Keep that spanking shit to the bedroom," Reid said. "Nobody wants to hear about that."

"Get your mind out of the gutter," Indina said.

"He can't," Toby said. "His mind is in the gutter so often that he's got a second mailing address there. 123 Gutter Street, USA."

"Now we see why you could never cut it as a comedian," Reid told him.

"Are we going to play volleyball?" Indina asked. "Because I didn't leave my very nice lounge chair to listen to you two trade insults."

"Bossy ass," she heard her brother say under his breath.

Indina kicked sand at him, then took up her position on her side of the net.

"Nuh uh," Griffin said. He pointed next to him. "That teammates thing doesn't apply only to work. Get over here."

"You don't even know if I can play," Indina said.

"I don't care. I want you on my team."

Her heart executed a disturbing little hop. Indina chose to ignore it as she dipped under the volleyball net and joined Griffin and Jonathan. Reid, Toby and Renee made up the other team. Jonathan's newest girlfriend, Kristy, decided at the last minute that she wanted to play.

Reid complained about his team being outnumbered, but it was soon apparent that Kristy was more of a liability than an asset. She screamed and ran from the ball whenever it came near her.

It didn't take long for Indina's competitive side to take over. The game quickly went from friendly family fun to all-out war against her brother and cousins.

It was also way more erotic than a friendly volleyball game should ever be.

She was hyperaware of every time Griffin's sweaty skin brushed against hers. They bumped into each other several times as they covered their half of the court, arms tangling, chests colliding. And each time they touched it set off another round of tingling in her belly.

It was silly. It wasn't as if his body was a mystery to her. She'd had her way with him for the better part of eight months. Yet, something about this felt different. They'd shared more than just their bodies last night. For the first time since they began sleeping together, they'd shared their minds. Learning about Griffin's work in Ghana, and his dreams of opening his own small engineering firm, had triggered a change in the way she saw him.

How had she not anticipated this happening when she invited him to join her on this cruise? She should have known that introducing him to her family, giving him just this tiny peek into her world outside of work, would change the dynamic of their arrangement.

She still wasn't sure how she felt about it. She shouldn't want this, but Indina couldn't deny how good it felt to lay next to him in bed last night. To feel his warm skin against hers instead of her cold pillow.

But was she ready to face the anguish that would come when things inevitably started to go south? Because it always went south. Despite all the arguments her brain continued to make, her heart knew the truth. If she couldn't make it work with Timothy—someone she'd given seven years of her life to, someone she thought she'd spend the rest of her life with—how could she ever think a relationship with Griffin would last?

She would enjoy her time with him on this cruise, but once they returned home, Indina knew she would have to draw the line.

Their volleyball game continued to be ultra-competitive, even though both teams insisted that it was all in good fun.

"Hell yeah! Good job," Griffin yelled after Indina set the ball up for him to spike it one last time. The match ended with their team winning by a landslide, despite having to navigate around Kristy.

Griffin came up to her and settled his hands at her waist. "How are you at bowling? Sykes-Wilcox is part of a league. We can use you."

"Bowling is boring," Indina said.

"Boring? That's only because you've never bowled with me."

"And you know how to make bowling more enjoyable?"

He leaned over and whispered in her ear, "I know how to make *everything* more enjoyable."

He trailed his fingers across her ribcage, and it was as if her one-piece bathing suit wasn't even there. Indina sucked in a swift breath as a million butterflies took flight in her belly.

The overwhelming urge to kiss that smile on his lips sent a jolt of alarm rocketing through her. She took a step back.

"I…uh…I need to…" She pointed toward the beach chairs. "I need to check on Sienna. Make sure she doesn't need anything."

She nearly tripped in the sand in her haste to leave the volleyball area.

What in the hell was happening here? Had she almost kissed him?

Girl, get a grip on yourself!

Indina had decided from the very beginning that kissing on the mouth crossed a boundary she was not willing to cross. She didn't have a problem sharing her body from the neck down, but the neck up?

No. *Hell* no!

That required a level of intimacy she wasn't ready to engage in. It mandated that she allow herself to be vulnerable, and she just wasn't there yet.

Maybe one day she could open herself up to going through all the things that were required to make a real relationship work, but after investing so much of herself into two long relationships that had come up short, Indina wasn't sure it was worth the hassle.

Why were all these damn feelings pushing their way into her head? Talk about ruining a good thing. She couldn't just continue to enjoy the great sex. Her stupid ass emotions had to worm their way into the situation.

Indina was spared from further uncomfortable run-ins with Griffin after Toby and Reid convinced him to join them on the Jet Skis they'd rented. The trio didn't get back until minutes before the shuttles returned to bring them all back to the ship.

Once back onboard, Indina joined the rest of the Holmes women in one of the hot tubs they'd commandeered. She'd taken the coward's way out; sneaking out of their cabin while Griffin was in the shower. She didn't care. There were too many mixed up emotions going through her head where he was concerned. She needed some time away from it all.

She couldn't think of a better escape than soaking in a luxurious hot tub with a frothy beverage in her hand.

Indina took a sip of her piña colada before setting the plastic cup on the deck and resting her arms against the hot tub's edge. She threw her head back and let the sun beat down upon her face. It felt glorious with the cool breeze coming off the water.

"I can't believe I wasn't going to come on this cruise," she said. "It would have been my biggest regret of the year."

"Even bigger than those lime green skinny jeans you wore to Alex and Renee's Fourth of July picnic?" Sienna asked.

Indina stuck her tongue out at her.

"I don't know why you ever considered *not* coming on this cruise," Monica said. "I've been looking forward to this ever since Margo came up with the idea."

"Did someone talk Gerald out of paying for the entire thing?" Sienna asked.

Indina sat up in the hot tub. "Wait, Gerald wanted to pay for *every*one? All twenty-five of us?" She knew her aunt Margo's husband was loaded, but that was just crazy.

"Alex refused to let him do it," Renee said. "But Gerald can be just as stubborn as these Holmes men, so don't be surprised if you have a reimbursement from the cruise company on your credit card statement."

If he did, Indina would give the money right back to Gerald.

A thought occurred to her. Maybe she would get his permission to put it toward whatever she and her brothers finally decided to create to honor their mother's memory. They were still debating whether they should institute a scholarship fund, or some other kind of education-centered program. All they knew was that Diane Holmes's legacy needed to live on. They would need to settle on the details as soon as they returned home. Her mother's birthday was in a couple of months and Indina wanted everything in place by then.

She looked over at Willow after it occurred to her that the last couple of emails she'd sent her regarding the memorial had gone unanswered. That should have been Indina's first clue that something weird was going on with her sister-in-law.

"You sure you don't want to get in,

Willow?" Indina asked. She'd taken the deck chair next to Sienna, who couldn't get in the hot tub because of her pregnancy. "It's pretty nice in here."

Willow gave her a small smile and shook her head. "This is just fine."

The smile was encouraging, but Indina would have felt better if it had reached her sister-in-law's eyes. She wasn't sure what to make of Willow's subdued demeanor. Not that she had ever been outspoken. Her brother's petite wife had a calmness about her that Indina admired. But she could speak her mind when the situation warranted, which was one of the reasons she and Indina got along so well.

But something was off. The Willow she'd encountered on this cruise ship was not the woman she'd come to know over the past seventeen years.

"Oh, did I tell you all about my anniversary present from Alex?" Renee asked, grabbing everyone's attention. She beamed with excitement as she described how Alex had presented her with a surprise trip to the Blue Ridge Mountains, where the couple had been married four years ago. Indina had missed the wedding, yet another regret.

"He wanted to rent the cabin where we were married, but I told him that was way too big for just the two of us."

"Hey, Eli and I would be happy to come along," Monica said. "I would love to go back to that house."

"I think we should all go back to the house where you and Eli got married in the Virgin Islands," Sienna said. "Tell Alex to switch."

"Thanks, but no." Renee laughed. "This time it will be just me and my hubby. It's been ages since we've had quiet time together." She looked over at Sienna. "But we're both afraid we'll miss the new baby's birth."

Sienna waved off her concern. "It's not as if this is the first one. Little Jonah will be waiting for y'all when y'all get back."

"I thought you all weren't finding out the baby's sex!" Monica quickly pounced on her.

"We haven't. I just have a feeling that it's a boy," Sienna said.

"You've decided on Jonah for a name? I like that," Indina said.

"Zenobia picked it. Her Grandma Margo has been reading her stories from the bible, and Jonah and the Whale is her favorite so far."

Indina laughed as they all chimed in on potential names, just in case Sienna's hunch was wrong and she had a girl. She relished having these women in her life. As much as she loved being spoiled as the only girl in the family, she'd been jealous of her friends who had sisters.

Indina could still remember when Harrison had met and married Willow back when they were in college. Her sister-in-law had filled the void of growing up surrounded by testosterone. As each of her three cousins' wives were added to the family, the feeling just continued to grow. They were all the sisters she'd never had, and she couldn't be more grateful for them.

The discussion moved from baby names to the chaos of family life, and what Sienna could expect with the addition of yet another little one pitter-pattering around the house. They all laughed when Sienna mentioned that she and Toby had flipped a coin over diaper duty, and he'd lost.

As they chatted about the roles their husbands had all played in helping with their newborns, Indina felt a twinge of something that was so foreign to her she hardly recognized it.

Was that...*envy*?

No. It couldn't be. Why would she feel envious over something she was certain she didn't want or need?

She'd decided back in her twenties that she just wasn't the motherly type, and she was still one hundred percent okay with that. She excelled at being the world's best aunt. She didn't need anything more than that.

But the thought of having someone to come home to every day? Someone to sit with on a lazy Sunday afternoon and watch the world go by as they talked about the week ahead? Someone who joined her in the kitchen to cook the pre-portioned meals that were delivered every week, then sat with her at the bar in her kitchen to eat them?

Someone to wrap their arms around her as

she drifted to sleep every night. Someone who would still be there in the morning with his arms around her.

Indina refused to allow her eyes to close, because she knew if she did she would envision Griffin in that role.

But why did that have to be a bad thing? No matter how much she tried to deny it, Indina knew something had shifted over these past twenty-four hours. She'd gotten only the tiniest peek into the man Griffin Sims was outside of the workplace and his bedroom, and already Indina found herself wanting to know more. She wanted to know *so* much more.

Could she finally start to peel back that armor she'd been encapsulated in since Timothy left? Had enough time passed?

The thought of making herself so vulnerable frightened Indina to no end, but listening to the women in her family describe the joy they felt on a daily basis had her ready to reconsider. The payoff just might be worth facing her fear.

Maybe she could finally be happy again, something she could admit she hadn't been for a while now.

"Enough of all this chitchat," Monica said. "Can we please talk about the elephant in the room?"

All the women focused on Indina.

"What?" Indina asked.

"Oh, don't give me that. You show up here yesterday with this fine ass man that none of us knew about. Spill it," Monica said.

Indina shouldn't have been surprised. In fact, she was surprised she'd been able to go an entire twenty-four hours without the women in her family bombarding her with questions about her relationship with Griffin, especially Monica.

Her cousin's wife had tried setting Indina up with several of the doctors who worked with her at Methodist Memorial Hospital, where Monica was the chief ER attending physician. The first black woman to ever hold that position, thank you very much.

But not one of Monica's attempts at playing matchmaker had panned out. Actually, none of them had gone beyond the first date. When Indina backed out of a date with one of the top plastic surgeons in the city, who even *she* had to admit had been one of the most gorgeous men she'd ever encountered, Monica had thrown in the towel.

She stared at Indina now with marked curiosity.

Indina took another sip of her drink and let out a satisfied *ahhh*. "Okay," she said, setting the drink down. "What do you want to know?"

"How long have you two been dating?" Renee asked.

"How old is he?" Monica asked.

"Who cares about any of that?" Sienna said. "I want to know if the sex is good."

"Okay, yeah, that too," Monica said.

Indina burst out laughing. "First, he's thirty-eight, so not all that young. We met when I started working on a project for Sykes-Wilcox."

"How long have you two been dating?" Monica asked.

Indina hesitated. "We haven't really been dating." She turned to Sienna. "And to answer your question, the sex is freaking fantastic."

"Alright girl!" Sienna said. She held up her cup of fruit punch in salute.

Renee raised her hand. "Hold up. I'm confused. The two of you are not dating, but you're having fantastic sex?"

"What's confusing about that?" Sienna asked. "Every girl's got an itch. Indina found herself a hottie to scratch hers." She leaned over and held her hand up for a high-five. "More power to you."

"Is that really all it is?" Monica asked with a frown.

Indina hunched her shoulders and nodded.

"Well, that sucks," Monica said. "You two look so good together. I was hoping this was something real."

"Didn't you hear the woman?" Sienna asked. "It *is* real. It's really good sex." She pointed to Indina. "Give us some details."

"Oh, please don't," Renee said. "If this is going to turn into a sex convo I'm tapping out right now. I've been so exhausted with my new job that I'm never in the mood lately."

"Uh oh. Being a school principal is more work than you thought it would be, huh?"

Indina asked.

"So much more," Renee said. "By the time I get home, feed the kids, and help with homework, I just want to crawl into bed."

"Poor Alex," Monica said, not even trying to hide her laugh.

"Poor *me*," Renee said. "I'd love to get into bed and do something other than sleep, but Alex is just as exhausted as I am, especially with Holmes Construction's new expansion. We're just two sexless adults waiting for the day we both have the time and energy to get back to doing it."

"Toby and I will happily keep Sebastian in our cabin tonight if you two want to get your freak on," Sienna offered. "We already have two little ones in the cabin with us. We can make room for a third." She tapped Willow on the arm. "Athens can join us too."

"That's not necessary," Willow said. "Besides, my husband hasn't touched me in months." With that, she slipped on her sunglasses and rose from her chair. "I'll catch up with you all later."

There was complete silence as they all stared at Willow's retreating form.

"Okay, I wasn't going to say anything, but there's something going on with those two," Monica said. "They've barely talked to each other on this cruise."

Sienna leaned toward the hot tub. "I don't know the full story, but according to what

Jonathan told Toby, Harrison has been a pain in the ass at the office lately. Jonathan said just about anything sets him off."

"Has she said anything to you, Indina?"

Indina shook her head, still looking toward the door where her sister-in-law had disappeared. "No, but there's definitely something going on. I'm going to try to talk to Harrison."

Monica, Renee and Sienna all snorted at the same time.

"Good luck with that," Sienna said.

Indina recognized the exercise in futility that would be. But she had to do something. She couldn't sit back and watch silently as her brother and sister-in-law just ignored each other's existence. As a couple, they had been the very definition of relationship goals. If the romance had gone sour in Willow and Harrison's once storybook marriage, Indina didn't see the point in even trying to find real love again.

Griffin had just finished the cool down on the treadmill when someone tapped him on the shoulder. He turned to find Toby.

"Hey, what's up?" Griffin asked as he pulled out his ear buds.

"Getting in a workout even after all that hustle at beach volleyball today?" Toby asked.

He shrugged. "My body is used to ninety minutes of high intensity. If it doesn't get that, I start to feel sluggish."

"I know what you mean. I try to do at least an hour a day myself." Toby climbed onto the treadmill next to his and started it at a slow jog. "I also want to take advantage of this sight while I can," he said, gesturing to the floor-to-ceiling windows that afforded a panoramic view of the water.

"Yeah, this is a lot better than the view from the gym I currently use. It overlooks an alley."

"Alex's company just finished up an addition on the house. I convinced Sienna to let me change Zoey's old room into a home gym now that she'll be on the side with the new nursery."

"Let me know if you plan to offer memberships," Griffin said with a laugh.

"Family is always invited. You're on this cruise, which means you're practically family now." A sly grin curved up the side of Toby's mouth. "You know you kind of surprised us there. No one was expecting Indina to bring a...um, what do you two call each other?"

"We're coworkers," Griffin said.

His grin broadened. "Yeah, okay."

"No, really," Griffin said, though he felt like a fool trying to deny there was anything going on between Indina and himself. Her family wasn't stupid. As each hour passed, Griffin found himself wanting more and more to be a part of this family. Hell, maybe he could enlist their help. If they approved of there being a real relationship between them, maybe Griffin could finally convince Indina to see it.

Toby's phone buzzed.

"You've got service on this ship?" Griffin asked.

He nodded. "I'm paying an arm and a leg for the damn wifi, but I need to be connected at all times."

Griffin had learned from Indina last night that Toby was the mastermind behind singing sensation, Aria Jordan. The R&B star had just finished up a nationwide tour that had made headlines because of the number of arenas she sold out.

"Shit, I didn't realize it was this late," Toby said. "Reid wanted to get in a game of basketball up on Deck 12. You up for it?"

"Hell yeah," Griffin said. "This hour on the treadmill was just a warm-up."

He followed Toby out of the gym and up one flight of stairs to the top deck. It held an array of recreational activities, including a half-size basketball court, a tennis court, miniature golf, and even a rock-climbing wall. They really did have everything on this ship.

Eli and Alex were already there, along with Jonathan Campbell. A minute later, Indina's three brothers arrived.

"We had to drag this one from his computer," Ezra said, tipping his head toward

Harrison.

"Dude, why did you even bring a computer?" Eli asked.

"I told him not to," Jonathan said. "We both agreed to leave everything at the office. I'm not thinking about any of my cases this weekend."

"When would you have time? I'm surprised you were able to sneak away from Kristy long enough to play ball," Reid said.

Toby let out a disgusted snort. The look Jonathan shot his way was pure murder.

Griffin felt as if he was missing something.

"Are we going to do this, or what?" Harrison asked. "If not I can go back to the brief I've been working on."

Toby pointed to Indina's brothers. "Griffin, why don't you join them? It'll be one set of Holmes brothers, along with their future brother-in-law, against the other set of Holmes brothers."

Griffin held his hands up to correct him on that brother-in-law thing, but no one paid him any attention.

"If it's brothers and brothers-in-law, what does that make me?" Jonathan asked.

Toby looked over at him. "A confused jackass?"

"What the hell is up with you?" Jonathan asked, stepping up to Toby.

"Just play ball," Toby said.

"Please," Alex added. "Renee and I have a couples massage scheduled at the spa. I don't plan to be late."

Griffin stood next to Reid. He said, "About that future brother-in-law thing."

"Toby was just joking. We all know Indina's not marrying you or anybody else," Reid said. "You can guard Eli. But watch it. He uses his elbows a lot."

For a moment, Griffin was rooted where he stood.

She isn't marrying anybody?

It was way too early for marriage to even enter the equation for him. Hell, he just wanted to go out on an actual date with her. He thought all it would take was a bit more coaxing, especially after the fun they'd had dancing last night. Not to mention their conversation after they left the club.

But it seemed as if Indina's aversion to relationships ran deeper than he first thought. Apparently, it was known and accepted among her family.

Was it even worth it to try to build their relationship into something more?

Griffin had tried to convince himself that he was satisfied with the status quo, but deep down he knew that wasn't the case. Maybe if he was still in his twenties he would be okay with things remaining casual, but he'd outgrown that way of thinking a long time ago. He was ready for a relationship with substance.

He was suddenly faced with the question he'd been trying to avoid for months now. How much time was he willing to invest in something that may never become anything more than just a string of hookups? It didn't matter that they were extremely gratifying hookups. There came a time when you had to move beyond the superficial.

Griffin's gut tightened with unease as he realized that he'd finally reached that point. If Indina wasn't willing to move forward, he would have to move on.

She's willing.

Or at least she would be if he went about this the right way. He just had to convince her that they were worth taking a chance on.

The basketball game finally got underway, but it was quickly apparent that one set of Holmes brothers had an advantage over the other. Griffin looked on in amazement as Toby and Jonathan put on a basketball clinic, displaying NBA-worthy moves.

"Wait, wait, wait. Hold up," Ezra said, waving his hands to stop the game. He looked over at Harrison and Reid. "How did we fall for this?"

"Because we're suckers," Reid said.

"What's going on?" Griffin asked.

"Those two knuckleheads both played professional ball. We got suckered into this game."

Toby put his hands up. "Hey, it was your idea to play," he said to Reid.

"I say we take this to the miniature golf

course," Alex said.

"That's not fair either. Doc here plays more golf than any of us."

"Not anymore," Eli said. "Between work and the kids, I don't have time to even look at my clubs. I haven't played a round of golf in over a month." He clamped an arm around Harrison's shoulder. "That said, I could still kick all your asses."

Reid cupped his hand over his mouth and yelled, "Fightin' words."

Griffin chuckled as the trash talking moved from the basketball court to the miniature golf course. He'd been intimidated at the thought of hanging around the men in Indina's family, especially now that the nature of their relationship was known to just about everyone. Instead of roughing up the guy who was sleeping with their sister, Indina's brothers had embraced him. It had been so damn long since he'd felt the camaraderie and brotherhood he'd experienced today.

An ache grew in his chest as he thought about his own brother and how they used to engage in the same good-natured ribbing he'd witnessed today between Indina's siblings and cousins. They'd had their share of skirmishes while growing up, but he and Garland had been thick as thieves. These days they barely said two words to each other.

Griffin's throat tightened as the sad reality of what had become of his relationship with

Garland settled into his bones. He missed his brother. And he knew no amount of time he spent encroaching on Indina's family would make up for what he'd lost with his own flesh and blood.

At least he had these Holmes men for the weekend. He would shamelessly glom on to this feeling of brotherhood for as long as he could.

Their golf game ended with Indina's cousins still beating the pants off of him and her brothers, but Griffin figured this butt whipping wasn't nearly as bad as the one they would have gotten if they'd continued the basketball game.

"Remember, dinner is at seven-fifteen tonight," Harrison said. He pointed to Jonathan. "Try to make this one."

"Can't make any promises," he replied. "Kristy wants a candlelit dinner for two."

"It's probably better if you didn't bring her to dinner anyway," Toby said. "I don't think Sienna is comfortable being around that Kristy chick."

"Would you stop referring to her as that Kristy chick?" Jonathan said. "And maybe you should remind Sienna that I have a right to see whoever I want. Her sister is the one who left me, not the other way around."

Griffin looked back and forth between the two men, trying to figure out just what in the hell was happening here.

"Don't ask," Ezra said as he came up to him and clamped an arm around Griffin's shoulder.

"Step over here with me. I want to talk to you for a minute."

"Uh, sure," Griffin said. He hooked a thumb toward Toby and Jonathan, who were still going at it.

"Didn't I just say don't ask?" Ezra said. He blew out a sigh. "Very, *veeery* long story short, Jonathan used to be engaged to Sienna's sister, Ivana. She got cold feet and left the country a few days before their wedding."

"She left the country?"

Ezra nodded. "Pretty drastic, if you asked me. Jonathan didn't take it well. He then proceeded to sleep with half the single women in New Orleans to prove to everybody that he's over Ivana." Ezra shook his head. "He's not. Anyway, I wanted to talk to you about Indina."

Griffin's steps halted. "What about her?"

Ezra cocked his head toward the locker that stored the basketball and tennis gear. He sat and rested his elbows on his thighs.

"I don't want to sound like the overprotective brother here," he started.

Griffin folded his arms across his chest and rocked slightly on the balls of his feet. This was the conversation he'd been expecting from the get-go.

"But?" Griffin asked.

"Hear me out." Ezra held up his hands. "I don't want to get all up in your business or anything. I just want to know what your intentions are. It's been a while since Deenie brought anyone to meet the family."

Griffin stopped rocking. It was on the tip of his tongue to ask Ezra just *how* long it had been since she'd introduced a guy to the family. Instead, he asked, "So, what exactly do you want to know?"

"I just want to know if this is serious? And if it *isn't* serious, does Indina know that?"

"I'm not playing your sister, if that's what you're worried about."

"No, I don't think you're playing her, but I had to ask. You get that, right? I don't want her to get hurt," Ezra said.

He pressed his lips together. Griffin knew someone had hurt her. No one adopted such a negative attitude toward relationships as the one Indina held without good reason.

"This is about that Timothy guy Reid mentioned at dinner last night, isn't it?" Griffin asked.

"In a way," Ezra said. "Timothy pulled a fast one on us. The entire family liked him, but he turned out to be the worst kind of asshole. She wasted seven years on that guy. I had to stop Reid from kicking his ass the last time we saw him."

"Maybe you should have let him," Griffin said.

Ezra huffed out a laugh. "The only reason I didn't is because I knew Indina would have been upset about it. She doesn't like anyone else fighting her battles. By the way," Ezra continued. "Don't mention this conversation to her. There would be hell to pay if she knew we'd talked about this."

"Yet you still did, even though you know she wouldn't want you telling me any of this."

"I'd rather deal with the fallout than see Indina get hurt." Ezra's eyes turned earnest. "I worry about her. I've seen my sister with a broken heart, and I don't like it."

"I'm not going to break her heart," Griffin assured him.

He'd have to own a piece of her heart in order to break it.

Ezra stood and held his hand out. Griffin clasped his palm and gave his hand a solid shake.

"I hope things work out between you two," Ezra said. "Not that many boyfriends would agree to being stuck on a cruise ship with a bunch of people he just met. This took guts man." Ezra pointed at him. "Oh, and don't tell her that I called her Deenie either. She hates that."

"That sounds like blackmail material," Griffin said with a chuckle.

Ezra patted him on the back. "Oh, yeah. You fit right in with the Holmeses."

Griffin stared in bewilderment as he watched Ezra walk away. How was it that he had more members of Indina's family—people he'd met for the first time *yesterday*—welcoming him into their lives. Yet the woman he'd shared a bed with for the last eight months didn't seem inclined to go any further with him? What did he have to do to make her see that he deserved to be more than just her occasional hookup?

Later that night, as he buried his face between Indina's thighs, Griffin approached the task with single-minded determination, intent on making her screams reach new heights. Whenever they were together, his number one goal was always to make her come as many times as possible, but tonight it felt different, as if he had something to prove.

Maybe it was the irrational jealousy he'd been grappling with ever since he learned that her last relationship had lasted seven years. *Seven years.* Griffin felt compelled to prove that he was the best she'd ever had.

He worked her over frantically with his tongue and fingers, thinking that if he could bring her even more pleasure, maybe he could finally reach that place she kept just out of arms' reach. It wasn't hopeless. If this asshole Timothy had done it, Griffin figured he sure as hell should be able to convince Indina that she could trust him with her heart.

Her thighs clamped around his ears as he drilled his tongue inside her. She cupped the back of his head, tugging gently as she lifted her hips to meet his tongue's every thrust. Griffin felt her orgasm building and rubbed his thumb over her clit, pressing down on it at the last minute.

Indina's hoarse scream echoed off the walls. Her limbs continued to quiver as Griffin worked his way up her body. He peppered her skin with gentle kisses, relishing its smoothness, the slightly musky taste of her on his tongue. But, as usual, when he reached her face Indina didn't give any indication that a kiss on the mouth would be welcomed.

It was like a knife to the gut.

After all the intimate moments they'd shared over the last eight months, why couldn't she bring herself to do this one simple thing?

Indina collapsed onto her side of the bed and stared up at the ceiling.

"You know, if you charged women to do that, you could give up your engineering career entirely," she said.

"Except that I really like being an engineer. And charging women to do that happens to be illegal."

She lulled her head to the side and looked him up and down. "Oh, right. It is, isn't it?" She let out a sigh. "I guess I'm really lucky that I get to experience it for free."

Chuckling, Griffin rolled onto his side and traced the curve of her ear with his finger. Indina released another sigh and burrowed closer toward him. His breath hitched in his chest.

He thought about it for a moment before deciding to throw caution to the wind and just go for it. Reaching over, he pulled Indina to him and settled her back against his chest. He felt her stiffen before she released another of those languid sighs and relaxed against him.

Words could not adequately describe the elation and relief that rushed through him. Last night, he'd waited until she'd been sleeping for several hours before he'd pulled her against him. To hold her like this while she was awake? To be in this bed with her like they were a normal couple? Griffin couldn't think of the words to express how this felt.

Amazing? Unbelievable? Euphoric?

No, none of those fit. There were no words for this.

He'd known for a while that he was no longer satisfied with these stolen moments together. He wanted more. He just didn't realize *how much* he'd started to crave it.

But Griffin also knew that he was taking a chance if she pushed her. And that she could find someone else to satisfy her needs if he pushed too hard.

Another insane rush of jealousy flashed through him just at the thought of another man doing the things he did with her.

"What's wrong?" Indina asked, glancing over her bare shoulder.

"What's that?" Griffin asked.

"You just…growled," she said.

Great. He was turning into a caveman. "It's nothing," he said. He tucked his chin against her shoulder and kissed behind her ear. "That was a pretty cool surprise at dinner tonight," he said.

"Umm hmm," she murmured. He could hear the smile in her voice.

During the dessert portion of the dinner, Indina's cousins presented their stepfather with a family portrait that included him in the painting with the boys and their mother. Indina explained later that Alex, Eli and Toby had not been fully onboard when her Aunt Margo started dating Gerald Mitchell. Based on what Griffin witnessed tonight, whatever negative feelings the men once held for their stepfather had dissipated.

"I like your cousins a lot," Griffin said. "Your brothers too. Hanging out with them today was…it was nice," he said. "It reminded me of what it used to feel like back when I was close to my own brother."

Indina turned to face him. Her puckered brown nipple peeked just above the sheet she'd pulled over them, and Griffin's first instinct was to dip his head and suck it into his mouth, but she stopped him with her next question.

"Are you and your brother no longer close?" she asked. She quickly followed her question with, "You don't have to talk about it if you don't want to."

His aversion to discussing his estrangement from Garland must have shown on his face. Or maybe she could read minds.

No. If she could read minds, then she would know exactly how he felt about her. More than likely, it was his sudden silence that had clued her in.

But after spending the day with her family and trying his best to tamp down the envy he'd felt at the genuine love and togetherness they exuded, Griffin couldn't help but think about his own family. Maybe talking about it would help alleviate the ache that had been plaguing him for so long.

"My brother and I had a falling out a few years ago," he said. His mouth twisted in a grim frown. "Actually, it's been more like six years."

"Six years?" Indina pushed herself up on her elbows. "Is he your only brother?"

He nodded. "My only sibling."

"My brothers get on my last nerve, but I can't imagine not talking to them for six years."

"We've talked," he said. "But only the barest minimum—as in we've said hello the couple of times we've seen each other. We've both conveniently missed the last few holidays at my parents'."

Indina was quiet for a few moments. In a gentle voice, she asked, "What happened?"

The significance of her concern wasn't lost on him. This was new territory for them. In all the months they'd been sleeping together, she'd never shown much regard for his life outside of work. Just this small indication that she cared enough to want to know more gave Griffin hope. He decided to put it all out there. Maybe if he opened up to her, she would reciprocate.

"It started with my ex-wife, Jacqueline," he

said. "Before she was my wife, she was my brother's girlfriend."

Indina's eyes widened. "You married your brother's girlfriend?"

"It's not as if I stole her from him or anything. Garland and Jackie had broken up long before she and I started dating."

Indina shook her head. "That doesn't matter. She was still off-limits. At least that would have been the case with my brothers."

"Garland's reason for being upset had nothing to do with me moving in on his old territory or anything like that. He was upset because I didn't listen when he tried to steer me away from her. Jackie had cheated on him with another guy, and Garland warned me that she would do the same to me."

"But you didn't listen."

Griffin shook his head.

"So, did she?" Indina asked.

He nodded. "Yeah, she did."

There was a lot more Griffin could have divulged, but the thought of trudging through the mire of his toxic marriage made him nauseous.

"So, your brother was right to warn you," Indina murmured.

"He was. But I'm just too damn stubborn to admit it." He snorted. Then he shook his head. "I hate how much this has hurt our family, especially my parents. They've both pleaded with us to mend fences, but I just don't see it happening."

Indina stared at him for a moment before she pushed herself up and leaned back against the headboard. "For someone as smart as you are, I can't believe you could be such an idiot," she said. "Do you realize how ridiculous it is for both you *and* your brother to allow someone who isn't even in your life anymore—someone who hurt you both—to continue hurting you? Don't you realize how much power that gives your ex-wife? You're giving her the power to hurt your entire family. She doesn't deserve that."

Griffin exhaled a frustrated breath. He knew Indina was right. He'd said the same thing to himself more than once.

But he was also a stubborn son of a bitch. So was Garland.

"For years I've told myself that this is just the way it is," Griffin muttered.

"But it doesn't have to be this way."

He had to clear his throat before he finally said, "I know." Griffin felt physically ill as he finally came to terms with what he'd allowed to happen to his family. "I have no idea what's happening in my niece and nephew's lives. I've missed school plays and Little League games. I send birthday gifts, but other than those two Christmases that my mom guilted me into attending, I haven't had anything to do with my niece or nephew for four long years, and that kills me."

"That's tragic, Griffin."

"It is. And I don't want to live this way anymore." He looked into her eyes. "You know what made the difference? Being surrounded by your family. I've been so damn jealous of all of you since I boarded this ship. But I realize now that I don't have to be. I have my own family. All I have to do is stop being a jackass and reach out to my brother."

"Yes, you do," Indina said.

She trailed her thumb over his jaw before cupping his chin in her delicate fingers. Griffin closed his eyes and gloried in how amazing it felt to have her touch him like this. As if he meant more to her than just a good lay. As if she cared for him.

Didn't these last few minutes show just that? She cared about the state of his relationship with his family. She cared enough to see that he was hurting and want to fix it.

This was all he needed. This one small indication that she felt just the barest concern was enough. He could build on this. He could show her they were worth taking a risk.

"I can promise you that your family misses you more than you know," Indina continued. "My family drives me absolutely bananas at times, but I would not give them up for anything in the world. They mean everything to me."

"I can understand why," Griffin said. "They're pretty awesome."

She smiled. "The Holmes clan is growing on

you, huh?"

"Yes, they are." He looked her straight in the eyes. "Especially a certain Holmes."

He wanted to kiss her mouth. God, did he want that.

But if she rejected him right now it might literally kill him. Instead, Griffin tugged the sheet from her breasts, leaned forward and finally pulled that nipple that had been teasing him into his mouth. Indina released a low moan as she captured his head between her palms and threw her leg over his hip.

He lowered her onto the mattress and fitted himself between her thighs. Grabbing a condom from the pack he'd set on the bedside table, he rolled the latex over his erection, and commenced to doing what they did best.

Chapter Five

Indina stood off to the side and counted as, one by one, the Holmeses descended from the shuttle bus and made their way through the gate of the ruins at Dzibilchaltún. After a nearly hour-long drive out to the ancient Mayan site, everyone was ready to get out and stretch their legs.

"Parents, keep your children with you until I get a final headcount," Indina called out as they all entered the gate.

At breakfast this morning, Harrison had tasked her with distributing tickets and keeping a count of everyone for the first stop on today's excursion. Indina had started to argue, just on principal at being told what to do, but after all the work her brother had put into this trip, she decided to lay off him. Besides, she didn't want to add to whatever stress Harrison was under.

Indina and Griffin agreed to bring up the rear so they could keep an eye on everyone, while her father led at the front. Despite the fact that he was knocking on seventy's door, Clark Holmes had the stamina of a man in his fifties. He still religiously jogged five miles a day.

Indina had watched him over the course of

the past two days and had finally convinced herself that he was indeed going to be okay. She knew his eyes would never have the same spark they had when her mother was alive, but he seemed genuinely happy. Of course, nothing made her dad happier than being surrounded by family, so this cruise was like heaven on earth for him.

The entire clan trekked across the rocky dirt paths toward the main ruins site. Their guide, Iktan, had the distinction of being a direct descendant of the Mayan people, which he proudly shared with them once every ten minutes or so. Her dad called for everyone to hush while Iktan explained the construction of the centuries old stone temples. He described the serpent design that ran throughout several structures, eliciting *oohs* and *ahhs* from the children and even a few of the adults.

"I just helped lay the tile work in Mama's bathroom at the old house," Toby said in a hush tone. "I understand this kind of craftsmanship."

Eli stared at him with disgust for a moment before he said, "Shut up."

Indina bit her lip to stop herself from laughing.

They explored a few of the buildings, including a 16th Century Franciscan church, before Iktan guided them to a structure that he proclaimed was the most important on the site.

"This, my friends, is the Temple of the Seven Dolls." He described the seven tiny effigies that were discovered in the temple when it was excavated, thus giving it its name.

Iktan pointed to the two window cutouts on either side of a large doorway. "If you are here on the Spring and Fall equinox, you will see the sun shining directly in the center of these doorways. This signaled harvest time for the Mayan. To this day, people travel from all over the world to witness it."

"Can we come back to see it? " Her eight-year-old nephew asked.

Indina rubbed her hand over Athens's stubby hair. "Maybe you can convince your mom and dad to take another cruise next spring."

"Only if he does well in school," Willow said.

"That's a given," Indina replied. "He takes after his Auntie Indina."

Willow smiled at that, and it struck Indina how rare it was to see a genuine smile on her sister-in-law's face these days. How had it taken her so long to recognized that something was off with those two?

As they all returned to the main site, Indina kept her eyes on Harrison and Willow. The iciness between them was unmistakable. All the other couples held hands as they traveled over the crumbling limestone road leading back to the other structures, but Willow kept her arms crossed over her chest. When Harrison reached over to assist her across a particularly rough patch, she flinched and stepped out of his reach.

Indina wasn't the only one who noticed it. She caught Liliana rolling her eyes at her parents. After that, the fifteen-year-old's entire disposition changed. Her sullen expression remained as the guide pointed out the remaining structures on their tour. It made Indina wonder just how long this rift had been going on between her brother and sister-in-law.

Their tour ended at the Cenote Xlakah, an ancient freshwater pool in the heart of Dzibilchaltún. Harrison had told them all ahead of time that there would be an opportunity to swim, but Indina had had enough of the water with her dip in the hot tub yesterday. Instead, she and Griffin decided to climb one of the surrounding temples that overlooked the grounds.

"You go first," Griffin said.

She started up the steps and then looked over her shoulder at him. "I know you just want to look at my ass while I climb."

"I asked you to go first because I'm a gentleman," he said. "I don't have to play games in order to take a peek at your ass. I see it all the time."

Indina burst out laughing as she started up the steep step.

"Be careful," Griffin said, capturing her waist to steady her when she got tripped up on a step. His fingers spread over her stomach and he pulled her back against him. "You okay?"

"Yes," Indina answered. When he went to move his hand, she clamped onto it, holding it against her belly. "Thank you," she said.

Griffin brushed his lips against her ear again and whispered, "I'm here for you, Indina. You need to recognize that I'm always here for you."

A medley of hopefulness, desire and unease stirred within her belly.

Indina fought the temptation to be pulled in by those softly whispered words. She couldn't allow herself to fully digest his statement without comparing it to similar promises that had been whispered in her ear in the past. Promises made by men who eventually had *not* been there for her.

Yet, even as she struggled to remain indifferent, she recognized the futility in doing so. She could no longer remain indifferent where Griffin was concerned. They'd shared too much over these past couple of days.

Once they arrived at the top, Indina settled in next to Griffin, their thighs touching as they sat side-by-side, overlooking the grounds. Just the feel of his warm skin against hers coated her in a layer of comfort.

That was one of the things that had stood out the most in these last few days. She now recognized just how comfortable she was with him. It hadn't come as a complete surprise. That sense of trust had been there from the very beginning. She never would have approached him—never would have spent the past eight months in his bed—if she'd felt even a modicum of unease around him.

But over the past few days, she'd been forced to see Griffin outside of the mental box where she usually stored their relationship. He was so much more than just a coworker she just so happened to be sleeping with. He was both sweet and kind, and he had things going on in his life that she would have never guessed. Issues with his family that Indina felt compelled to help him work through. The fact that she hadn't been able to stop thinking about the rift between Griffin and his brother told her that she cared way more than she would have if he meant nothing to her.

It scared the hell out of her.

It scared her to think of how admitting she cared changed the dynamics of this entire arrangement. Caring added a layer of vulnerability Indina wasn't ready to accept, but it felt as if it was out of her hands.

She *did* care about him. Now she had to decide just what to do about that.

"Have I thanked you for inviting me to join you here?" Griffin asked.

Indina's lips tipped up in a smile "Yes, you have," she said. "Have I thanked you for coming?"

"Not sure if you said it with words, but that thing you did with your tongue last night was thanks enough."

She was a forty-two year old woman; she

would *not* blush.

Griffin's deep chuckle told her that it was too late. She was definitely blushing.

"Well, just in case I haven't said it in actual words, thank you for joining me," Indina said. "I've had a good time."

"Does it make you wonder how many good times we've missed because you're always so quick to leave me?"

"Griffin—"

"I mean it, Indina. Look at how much fun we had that first night when we went to that disco on the ship. There are clubs back home where we could hang out, have drinks, dance—although you may not want to be seen dancing with me in public."

She released a strained laugh. "It's not about your dancing."

"Then what is it?"

The sudden seriousness in his tone triggered her defensiveness. She tamped it down, and reminded herself that she was still in the driver's seat when it came to how their relationship operated.

"Griffin, we decided from the very beginning that we didn't want this to get too serious."

"That was eight months ago, Indina. And I'm not asking you to marry me, just to go out on an actual date with me."

She set her elbows on her thighs and ran her hands down her face. "Can we please not talk about this right now? I can't think about us," she said, pointing between the two of them, "when I'm still trying to figure out what's going on with Harrison and Willow."

Griffin frowned. "What do you mean? What's going on with Harrison and Willow?"

She lifted her shoulders in a hapless shrug. "I have no idea. What I *do* know is that something isn't right. The two of them have hardly talked to each other this entire cruise. And yesterday, while we were all hanging out in the hot tub, Willow made a comment that leads me to believe that she and Harrison have been having problems for a while."

"Either of them come to you about it?"

Indina shook her head. "I'm not surprised that Harrison hasn't said anything. He could be up to his neck in quicksand and would insist he doesn't need help getting out of it. But I thought Willow and I were close enough that she would confide in me if she and my brother were having problems."

"Maybe they want to work it out for themselves."

"But what if it's too serious for them to try to work it out for themselves?" She looked over at him. "They have children, Griffin. It's already affecting Liliana. I saw her watching her parents earlier. I could tell that she's bothered by it." Indina shoved her hands in her hair and massaged her scalp. "If those two end up getting a divorce, it will destroy those children."

"Don't get ahead of yourself, Indina. There are a lot of stages between giving each other the silent treatment and filing for divorce. Believe me, I've been there."

She stared at his strong profile and was struck again by how much she didn't know about him.

"So it wasn't just the cheating that signaled the end of your marriage?" she asked.

"No, it was a lot more than that." He set his elbows on his thighs and clamped his hands together. Looking straight ahead, he said, "Earlier, when we were walking on the beach. Do you remember what you said about your parents' marriage? About how perfect they were for each other?"

Indina nodded. She and Griffin talked about the classic love affair her parents shared as they'd strolled along the shoreline this morning.

"My marriage was the exact opposite," he said. "It was toxic from the very beginning. The more I've thought about it, the more I've come to realize that Jacqueline probably only married me to get back at Garland. When she realized that it didn't matter to him, that's when she was done with me. It just took me a while to catch on."

Indina reached over and ran her fingers along his forearm, compelled by the need to provide him just a small bit of comfort. He seemed to glom on to it, covering her hand with his.

"How did you find out about her

infidelity?" she asked.

"I hired someone to follow her." His derisive snort told Indina everything she needed to know about how that turned out. "It was a waste of money," Griffin said. "It's not as if she tried all that hard to hide it. They went to the same hotel every week. Even charged it to our joint credit card a couple of times."

"Talk about ballsy," Indina said. "It's as if she wanted you to find out."

"She did. That's why she chose a hotel that was just a few blocks from my old job back in Milwaukee."

"Is that why you've always insisted we go to your house instead of a hotel?" Indina asked.

He lightly squeezed her hand. "That has nothing to do with it. I want you in *my* bed. You belong in my bed. *Only* my bed."

Why did that hint of possessiveness turn her on so damn much? Normally she would balk at the insinuation that she belonged to any man, but not today. Today, her nipples drew tight and achy just at the thought of Griffin only wanting her for himself.

"So, what happened when you finally confronted your ex with the evidence?" she asked.

"I didn't. At least not right away." He blew out a weary breath and ran a hand down his face. "I should have. Maybe it would have prevented me from doing what I eventually did do." Before Indina could voice the question,

Griffin continued. "The weekend after the investigator emailed me the pictures, I went out with some friends to get my mind off of the fact that my marriage was essentially over. I drank way more than I should have, but not enough to be incapacitated or not know what I was doing…"

She was almost afraid to ask. "What did you do?"

He paused for a moment. "Made eye contact with this random woman at the club, followed her into the bathroom and had sex with her." He shook his head. "I don't even know her name. Never bothered to ask." He sucked in a deep breath. "It was the absolute lowest point in my life." The pain in his voice touched her deep down in her bones.

"Griffin," she whispered.

"I knew I was doing it to get back at Jacqueline," he continued. "I'd convinced myself that she deserved it. But stooping to her level was never the answer. I can't tell you how much I hate that I allowed myself to become the kind of man who would do something like that."

Of all the things he could have admitted to doing, that was never even on the list. Granted, this was the first time they'd ever discussed something so deeply personal, but she and Griffin had hung out together with their coworkers enough times for her to know that he prided himself on being honest and upstanding. It was one of the things Indina most admired about him. Committing adultery, even though it was to get back at an adulterous spouse, didn't jibe with what she knew about the man sitting next to her.

"I guess it's understandable that you would—"

"No, it isn't," Griffin said. "I refuse to make excuses for what I did. It was wrong. I own up to that."

"Tell me the divorce came quickly after that," Indina said.

"It did. Once I showed her the pictures, she knew she couldn't deny it."

"Did you ever tell her what you did?"

He shook his head. "No. I did it to hurt her, but I soon recognized that she didn't love me enough to be hurt by it." He looked over at her. "I never told anyone what I did. Not even the friends I went out with that night. This is the first time I've talked about it in six years."

Indina had trouble swallowing past the knot in her throat. Knowing that he trusted her with something so personal, so painful, humbled her like nothing had before.

"I'm so sorry, Griffin." She wrapped her hands around his muscular bicep and rested her head on his shoulder.

"Does this—" He cleared his throat. "Does this change the way you see me?"

Indina looked up at him. If the look in his eyes didn't tell her how much her answer meant to him, the anxiety bracketing his mouth would have.

She shook her head. "No," she answered softly. "Actually, that isn't true. I'm touched that you trusted me with something so personal."

Indina questioned her next move before she made it. It was the one thing she'd avoided in the last eight months. But as she stared into Griffin's eyes nothing felt more right. She captured his jaw in her palm and touched her lips to his. Griffin's groan was audible. Indina felt his body shudder as he gently glided his lips over hers.

She understood the significance of this moment, what it meant to finally open herself up enough to kiss him on the lips. Instead of scaring her, it made her even bolder. She opened her mouth and pulled his tongue inside. And wondered why it had taken her so long to taste his kiss.

She reveled in the pleasure that seized her body, the unmitigated bliss that captured her senses as Griffin's tongue tangled with hers. It had been so long since she'd allowed herself to be so thoroughly kissed. She'd missed it. This feeling of closeness, of intimacy, of trust.

It didn't come as a surprise that Griffin's kiss surpassed any other she'd ever known. As with everything else, he seemed to know exactly what she craved.

"Wait until you're in your room to do that!"

Indina jerked back. She looked down and saw Ezra waving at them.

"Come on," her brother called. "It's time to go."

Indina stood, but before she could take a step further, Griffin pulled her to him and gave her another swift kiss.

His intense gaze arrested the air in her lungs. "I could kiss you for the rest of my life," he said before finally releasing her.

Indina tried to wipe away the doubt that slowly swept over her as they headed back toward the shuttle buses. After they wrapped up their visit to Dzibilchaltún, they toured the ruins at Chichen-Itza. Before they left the second site, Monica announced that they were going to have a late lunch of authentic Mexican food at a restaurant in the capital city of Merida. Alex complained about spending money at a restaurant when they could eat on the cruise ship for free, but Renee quickly put an end to his protest.

When they arrived at the restaurant, Monica instructed them to all gather on the sidewalk. She called for Gerald to join her in front of the restaurant's entrance.

"On behalf of my generous father-in-law, I'd like to welcome you all to the official Holmes Family Reunion Celebration. Gerald rented out the restaurant for the afternoon." She turned to Margo. "Don't bother fussing with him over it. He wanted to do it and would not take no for an answer."

They were greeted by the restaurant's

owners, an older couple who had been married so long they looked alike. The space was decorated with balloons, streamers and a banner welcoming the Holmes Family. There was even a mariachi band.

They were all seated at a long set of tables that ran the entire length of the dining area.

Indina's mouth literally watered as platters of succulent dishes were laid before them. Pork wrapped in banana leaves and cooked underneath hot coals, pickled red onions, beans and rice, fresh handmade tortillas and everything you could think of for an authentic Mexican feast.

Once they'd all eaten first and then second helpings, the tables were moved to the side and the mariachi band started up with more lively music. The children were the first to the dance floor, but they were soon followed by the elders of the family. Indina could hardly catch her breath as she watched her dad take fifteen-year-old Liliana—the only Holmes child who was *not* dancing—and drag her to the floor. It took only a few moments before her niece went from surly teen to cheerful and carefree.

Indina spotted her brother sitting at one of the tables in the corner, staring at the dance floor. She walked over to where he sat and pulled a chair up next to his. She bumped his shoulder. "That should be you out there with Lily."

Harrison snorted. "As if she would have

gone out on that dance floor with me. Not in this lifetime."

"So she likes her grandpa more than she likes her dad," Indina said with a shrug. "Doesn't surprise me one bit."

"Thanks a lot."

"Oh, come on." Indina laughed at his incredulous tone. "She's a teenager. She likes everyone more than she likes her dad."

"Except when it's time for her to go to the mall," Harrison said. He nudged his head to where their father and Liliana were doing some kind of two-step. "It's good to see him having a nice time. This cruise was good for him."

"It was good for the entire family," Indina said. She glanced over at her brother, debating whether or not she should broach the subject of him and Willow. It probably wasn't the best time to talk about it, but the ship docked in New Orleans in the morning and who knew when she'd have Harrison's ear again.

Anticipating her brother's reaction, Indina opted for a humorous, wise-ass approach. Maybe it would take the edge off this sensitive topic.

With a light chuckle, she bumped her shoulder against his again, and said, "Soooo, I don't want to get all up in your business, but your wife mentioned that your bedroom has been pretty quiet lately. You don't need the little blue pill do you?"

Harrison's gaze swiftly shot to her, his eyes

wide. "She said what?"

Okay, so maybe humor wasn't the way to go. She turned to him, and in a lower voice, said, "If I remember her words correctly, she said you haven't touched her in months. So?" Indina prompted when he didn't say anything.

Lines of tension bracketed Harrison's mouth. "I'm not having this conversation with my little sister."

"Oh, please." Indina snorted. "I'm younger than you by fourteen months. And I started having sex even before you did."

"I'm sure as hell not having *that* conversation with you," Harrison said. "Especially since it happened to be with my best friend at the time."

Indina smiled. "Marshall was a sweetheart. I need to check in on him. I heard that he and Robert are thinking about adopting another kid."

"They already have. A little girl named Ashley," Harrison said. "They asked me to be the godfather." He looked over at her. "Are we done here?"

"No," Indina said, serious now. "I want to know what's going on with you and Willow? Is this your regular little husband and wife spat, or is it something more serious?"

"It's nothing that you should be concerned about."

"Well I *am* concerned, especially after noticing the way Lily looked at you both earlier at the ruins." Her brother's eyes widened with surprise. Indina shook her head. "Really, Harrison? You don't think your kids pay attention? They both do, and I'll bet they both see that something isn't right between the two of you."

"It's...I don't even know," he said. He ran a hand down his face. "You want to know the truth? That's it. I have no idea what's happening with Willow. But it's none of your business, so stay out of it." His tone brooked no argument. "I mean it, Indina. I don't need you sniffing around my marriage. Let me figure out whatever is going on with my own damn wife."

"Fine." She put both hands up, but then clamped a hand on his forearm. "Just know that I'm here if you need to talk about anything. I love both of you, Harrison. And you know those kids mean the world to me. I don't like to see them hurting and if they see the two of you unhappy, then they will be unhappy." She gave his arm a light squeeze. "Promise you'll come to me if you need me."

He gave her the barest nod before gesturing to the dance floor. "Can we go back to enjoying ourselves now?"

"Do you call what you were doing before 'enjoying' yourself? Maybe you *do* need some lessons on how to loosen up."

"Forgive me for not being the social butterfly that your boyfriend is," he said, pointing to where Griffin was stuck between

Margo and Sienna in the conga line. Harrison chuckled. "He sure fits in with this family, doesn't he?"

"Yes," Indina murmured. "He does."

She spent the next hour questioning exactly why she didn't correct Harrison when he referred to Griffin as her boyfriend. At the same time, Indina ruminated on just how well Griffin *did* seem to fit in with the Holmeses. Her aunt Margo was undoubtedly charmed by him, and when her nephew discovered Griffin was a huge Star Wars fan—something Indina had not known either—Athens bombarded him with questions about his favorite characters.

When the image of Griffin at a Holmes family picnic, or sitting at the huge dining table at Christmas, enjoying dinner with her family didn't immediately rattle her, Indina knew something had fundamentally changed.

And *that's* what *really* rattled her.

She'd spent the past two years convincing herself that she was okay with never being in a relationship again. Yet, she could picture all too well what it would be like to start a relationship—a *real* relationship—with Griffin Sims. That fear of being vulnerable, of opening herself up to the hurt and humiliation she'd experienced in the past? It didn't seem to matter anymore. None of it was as strong as the pull to recreate moments like this with Griffin in the future.

Indina thought back to their walk on the

beach, when they'd discussed her parents' marriage and how, for the barest second, she'd wondered if she could have that kind of love with Griffin. She knew the danger in indulging such thoughts, yet there they were, stealthily intruding, giving her a sense of hopefulness she had not allowed herself to feel in so very long.

The fear of trusting even that small bit of hope she felt left Indina breathless. It terrified her.

A few moments later, Monica reluctantly cut off the band's play, announcing that they all would have to board the shuttles in the next ten minutes in order to make it back to the cruise ship before it departed. Despite the restaurant owners' insistence that they leave everything as is, everyone pitched in to return the tables to their rightful places and pick up as much mess as possible.

"The shuttles can only stay parked at the curb for a few minutes, so we need to be out there waiting for them," Monica said.

As everyone started filing out of the restaurant, Griffin sidled up next to Indina, his dark brown skin flush after all the dancing and laughing.

"You Holmeses know how to a party," he said.

Indina sent him a pensive smile, still shaken by the conflicting thoughts warring in her brain. Apparently, her smile wasn't enough to hide her emotions.

Griffin's brow furrowed. "Hey, are you okay?"

"I'm fine." She had to clear the lie from her throat before she could continue. "I'm happy you're having such a good time with my family. Enjoy them while you can."

His head snapped back. A mask of hurt and confusion shrouded his face.

"Okay, people, let's board the shuttle," Monica called.

"Indina?" Griffin reached for her, but she stepped out of the way.

"We should go," she said as she started for the shuttle.

She couldn't even look him in the eye.

The Holmes crew had taken over the left side of the small lounge aboard the cruise ship. As they relaxed on the plush sofas and chairs, sipping on a fresh round of drinks and laughing at Reid's questionable dance moves from this afternoon's party, Griffin quietly basked in this sense of togetherness...while he still had the chance to enjoy it.

Indina's words from this afternoon continued to churn in his gut.

He'd questioned her once they arrived back on the ship, but she'd brushed it off, claiming she was just worried about Harrison and Willow and hadn't been thinking clearly. Griffin believed that as much as he believed Reid was a potential contender for *Dancing With The Stars*. He knew damn well Indina meant for things to go back to the way they were once they returned to New Orleans, but there was no way Griffin could go for that. Not anymore. Not after being immersed in this big, boisterous, amazing family for the last three days.

He wanted them in his life. Permanently.

In the same way he wanted *her* in his life.

The thought of falling back into their old hookup routine made him physically sick. How could she think that would be enough for him after the time they'd spent together this weekend?

Why do you think she would want more?

Indina had never been anything but straight with him. She'd never led him on, or pretended to want anything other than the arrangement they'd agreed upon eight months ago.

That still didn't change his feelings. Griffin could not — *would* not — go back to the way things were. That applied to more than just his relationship with Indina.

Earlier, while soaking in the fun of this afternoon's celebration at the Mexican restaurant, Griffin made the decision to finally reach out to his brother. Witnessing the way these Holmeses argued one minute then joked with each other the next, showed Griffin that this wound between him and his brother had festered for way too long. He wouldn't allow his stubbornness to keep him away from his family any longer. He was going to extend an olive branch to Garland as soon as he returned to New Orleans. Whether or not his brother accepted it was still a question, but Griffin vowed to do his part.

But even if he did make things right with Garland, he knew it wouldn't curb his desire to be a part of *this* family. Yet, Griffin knew belonging to the Holmeses was only a small part of what was driving him.

He wanted Indina. He'd wanted her for months. He wanted *all* of her, not just her body. Griffin dreaded even thinking about the conversation they must have, but it was their last night on the cruise. He refused to step foot off this ship without telling Indina where he stood.

It was all or nothing. Either she agreed to being more than just the occasional bed partner, or they broke things off completely.

Pain pierced his chest just at the thought of his time with her coming to an end, but Griffin could no longer stomach being used as just a means of getting off. If Indina could not see that they deserved to be an actual couple, then he was done.

Toby called Griffin over to finish a discussion they'd started with Jonathan earlier today about ideas he wanted to incorporate into the new club he was opening in New Orleans's Warehouse District. A few minutes later, he noticed Indina rise from the chair where she'd been sitting most of the night. Her eyes connected with his. It was the first time she'd looked his way since they'd arrived in the lounge. Griffin didn't know what to make of the despondent expression clouding her eyes. He heard her say to Monica that she was tired and turning in for the night before walking out of the lounge.

After another twenty minutes, he couldn't take it anymore. He made a quick excuse about turning in early and made his way to their cabin. He walked in to find it empty.

Dammit.

He was just about to go back out and search for her when he caught sight of Indina's feet propped up on the balcony railing. Relief crashed into him, but it was quickly replaced with a feeling of dread. It was time they had the conversation that had been months in the making.

Griffin walked over to the sliding glass door and pushed it further open. Indina sat with her hands folded over her stomach, her head tilted back. The slight breeze off the water blew the hair around her face. The soft crush of the waves against the ship's hull provided an eloquent song to the portrait of serenity she presented.

But Griffin could tell it was just a facade. The tension lines bracketing her mouth betrayed what was really going on inside her head. He knew because he'd been dealing with those same feelings since they left the restaurant in Merida.

"We need to talk," Griffin said.

She didn't move. Didn't open her eyes. If not for the small dip in her brow Griffin would have wondered if she'd heard him at all.

"We need to talk about what you said as we were leaving the restaurant this afternoon. I know you don't want to discuss it. That's why you've been in this sulky mood tonight, right?"

She remained silent for several moments more. His chest tightened with each second that ticked by. Finally, she raised her head and looked at him.

"A little," she admitted. "I know what you're going to say and I'm not sure I'm ready to hear it."

"What am I going to say?"

The words came out in a whisper. "That you want a real relationship."

"Would that really be so bad?" Griffin came farther out onto the veranda, taking the other chair. He clasped his hands together and stared out at the water. "You say it as if the thought of starting a real relationship with me is the scariest thing on earth." He turned to her. "Why is that, Indina?"

She pulled her bottom lip between her teeth. The tormented look in her eyes gutted him to the point where he nearly backed off, but Griffin steeled himself against the urge to halt the conversation. They were in the midst of a pivotal moment. There was no going back.

"I don't know," Indina finally answered.

"I'm just...I don't know how to feel about this, Griffin. I liked what we were doing before. I liked it because it was safe."

"And you think being in a real relationship with me won't be?"

"It hasn't worked out for me in the past."

He curbed the sudden impulse to lash out at her for comparing him to the men who'd hurt her before.

"I deserve a chance to prove that I'm better than the guys you've been with in the past," Griffin said.

"I know," she said. "I'm sorry. I just..." She held her hands out, pleading with him to understand. "What about all the things that could go wrong? What if we discover that we don't work as a couple? How could we ever go back to just being friends?"

He stared at her for a moment before he said in a soft voice, "You do realize we aren't friends now, don't you?"

Instant shock registered in her light brown eyes.

"We *are* friends," she said.

"No, we're not. We're coworkers who fuck on the weekends."

Her entire body went rigid. Griffin started to apologize for his crudeness, but decided against it. Maybe the shocking language would get through to her since his subtle hints sure as hell hadn't.

"Indina, before this weekend I didn't know

how many siblings you had. I didn't know your favorite color, or that you liked bananas, or that you were a cheerleader in high school. I learned more about you in the past three days than I'd learned in over eight months of sleeping with you. Friends talk to each other about what's going on in their lives outside of work. We don't do that."

He reached over and gave her arm a fleeting caress with the backs of his fingers.

"But I *want* to," Griffin said softly. "I want to know everything there is to know about you."

Her bottom lip started to tremble. She pulled it between her teeth.

"What scares you so much?" Griffin asked.

"Getting hurt," she admitted in a small voice. She released a deep breath and lifted her shoulders in a hapless shrug. "That's what scares me, Griffin. Once there's a real emotional connection, you'll have the power to hurt me."

"I won't hurt you, Indina. I would never hurt you."

"You don't know that. Look at what happened between you and your first wife."

He pulled his hand away and stood. "Don't do that," Griffin said. "I didn't tell you about that just so you could turn around and use it against me."

"But it's a valid point."

"No, it isn't. What we have could never be as toxic as what I had with Jackie. You're nothing like her, and I'm not the man I was back when I was married to her.

"Why are you so afraid to even consider that maybe things could work out between us? That we could have the happily ever after? It's not unheard of, Indina. Just look at all the people in your family."

"Like who? Like Harrison and Willow?" she asked. "They can barely stand to talk to each other. Do you want to know about Alex and his first wife, Chantal? She died in a car wreck with her lover when Jasmine was just a baby. How's that for your happily ever after?"

"And you don't think Alex has found happiness with Renee?" Griffin asked. "And what about all the others? Your cousins and their wives? Your Aunt Margo and Gerald? Your own parents?" he asked. "We could be one of those. Or maybe we won't, but damn, Indina, just give us a chance." Griffin ran his hand down his face. "Look, I know when we started this, neither of us were ready for a relationship—"

"Which is why what we have going right now is perfect."

"Except it's no longer enough for me," he said. "I want more."

She pulled her sweater more securely around her. "So what are you saying? Is this an ultimatum? Either I agree to enter into a real relationship with you or I find myself another fuck buddy?"

The jealousy that came over him at the thought of her lying next to some other man at night was thick enough for Griffin to choke on.

Indina closed her eyes and pitched her head back. With another frustrated breath, she said, "If I'd known this is what would come of this weekend I never would have invited you to come on this cruise."

Her words hit him like a baseball bat to the chest.

"That didn't come out right," Indina said.

Griffin just stared at her. He had to clear his throat before he could speak.

"Do you care for me at all? Do you have any feelings for me outside of what I do for you in bed, or am I just a good lay to you?"

She hesitated a second too long. It was all the answer he needed. He pushed away from the railing and went back into the cabin.

"Griffin," Indina called after him, but he didn't stop walking. Not until he reached the top deck and found himself face up on a lounge chair, staring mindlessly at the millions of stars in the sky.

When he returned to their cabin hours later, Indina was already asleep. For the first time in eight months they slept in the same bed without making love.

Chapter Six

"What about Diane's Daughters?"

"That's stupid," Ezra said. "Mom only had one daughter."

"But the foundation will be for girls, so in a sense they're all mom's daughters." Reid tapped the side of his head. "Think outside the box, man."

"The Diane Holmes Foundation is just fine," Ezra said.

"The Diane Holmes Foundation sounds boring. Hey." A piece of popcorn came flying at Indina's head. "You plan to have some input or what?" Reid asked.

Indina jumped. "Huh?"

Her brother threw another popcorn kernel at her head. "If you came here to just stare into space you could have stayed your ass home," Reid said. "And where in the hell is Harrison? He should be here. He's the one doing all the legal stuff for Mom's foundation."

"Shhh," Ezra told Reid as he looked over his shoulder. "Don't talk so loud. I think Dad's in the next room. He'll hear you."

"Maybe he should," Reid said. "I still think if we're going to set up a foundation in Mom's name, he should have some input."

"He *will* have input. We just want to have the initial groundwork laid so we can present it to him on Mom's birthday. You know that's going to be a hard day for him." Ezra turned to Indina. "And he's right. We could use your input here. Have you been paying attention at all to this conversation?"

She could lie and say that she had, but Indina had only been listening with half an ear. "I'm sorry," she said. "What were we discussing?"

"The foundation," Reid said.

She rolled her eyes. "I know we're discussing the foundation. Have we established each of our roles yet? That would prevent us all from working on the same thing at the same time."

"Harrison is handling all the legal stuff, and I'm going to deal with the PR," Ezra said.

"We haven't even decided on an official name yet," Reid interjected. "It's too early to think about PR."

"It's never too early to think about PR," Ezra said. "And the name will be The Diane Holmes Foundation."

"Diane's Daughters is better," Reid said.

"Okay, okay." Indina put her hands up. "We first have to decide what our initial goal will be. We know we want to build this into a foundation to help at least one student from the New Orleans area go to medical school—"

"Just one?" Reid asked.

"Of course we want to eventually help more than just one, but we have to have a realistic starting point. I think Harrison's first suggestion is still the way to go. We set up the foundation and sponsor a scholarship of $10,000 to a student planning to study cardiology, and who is specifically planning to deal with heart disease in the black community."

"And I still think there needs to be a physical component. Something that would look good in print," Ezra said. "Maybe we can partner with a local clinic to do free health screenings, or hold seminars on how heart disease affects black women. Scholarships are great, but they don't create the same visuals as a room full of people getting checked out by doctors and nurses. We need to show people that we're actually doing stuff. That kind of PR is what brings in donations."

"Here he goes again," Reid said, rolling his eyes. "Always on this PR trip."

Ezra pointed to him. "I told your ass—"

"Hey, when did you all get here?" They all jumped at the sound of their dad's voice as he entered the kitchen. "I guess this is what I get for letting my grown kids all keep their house keys." He came around the table and pressed a kiss to the top of Indina's head. "You don't have to work?" He looked around at his sons. "Do any of you work?"

"I'm waiting to hear from Alex before I go back to the work site," Reid said. "The construction job we've been working on had a bunch of rain delays so the crew is behind. We're supposed to start on the plumbing today, but who knows."

"Didn't one of your foreman leave? Have you all found someone to replace him?" Ezra asked.

Reid shook his head. "I've given Alex the names of a few people to interview, but he's picky as hell when it comes to Holmes Construction. He's not going to bring in just anybody."

"And he shouldn't," their father said. "If it's got the Holmes name on it, it needs to be held to a certain standard." He gave Indina's shoulder a squeeze. "And what about you? What are you doing here on a Tuesday afternoon instead of at your office?"

"I'm working from home today," Indina said.

"My home?"

"Hey, it was my home for eighteen years," she said with a laugh. "And I'm here so that I could help these two gang up on you about flying out to San Diego with your Navy buddies," Indina said.

"Oh, don't start that again."

"It would be good for you, Dad."

He pointed to a domed cake holder next to the coffee pot. "Have you all had a piece of that cake on the counter? Mrs. Johnson brought it over. It's good."

"That's the lamest dodge I've ever heard in my life," Ezra said as he rose from the table. "But it worked." He grabbed a plate and sliced himself a piece of cake. He pointed his fork at their dad. "Hey, why didn't you ask me why I'm here instead of at work?"

"Because he doesn't think you have a real job," Reid said.

"Stop that, Reid," their Dad said.

Ezra's work situation remained a sticky subject. Although Indina knew Reid's jab held no malicious intent, their dad wouldn't allow anyone to needle Ezra over his termination from the newspaper where he once worked.

She, however, still had a bone to pick with her brother.

"Apparently Ezra's job is harassing Councilmember Arnold," Indina said. "I thought I asked you to leave Mackenna alone?"

"I'm not harassing her," Ezra said. "I'm researching a story."

"You're being a pain in the ass to one of my dearest friends. I'd appreciate it if you'd stop."

Her dad walked over to Ezra and clamped a hand on his shoulder. "If your brother thinks there's something going on, then my bet's on him. I read that piece you wrote about the new zoning being done in the city. You got under a lot of people's skin with that one."

"Yeah, well, it isn't juicy enough to get me the kind of coverage that's going to pay the bills," he said. "These days I spend more of my time teaching journalism than actually practicing it. Speaking of teaching, I need to head home so I can try to make a dent in the papers I have to grade." He pulled a roll of foil from the cabinet and wrapped up a second piece of cake. "The new department head is a hard ass about things like that. I think he's just sucking up to the president of the college."

"Ezra, can I get your word that you're going to leave Mack alone?" Indina asked.

"No way." He shook his head. "I know she's your friend and all, but there's something shady going on with Mackenna Arnold and her husband."

"He is her ex-husband," Indina said pointedly.

"Doesn't matter. They were married at the time all this stuff I'm digging up happened. She had to have known and was complicit." He opened the door that led to the back steps, but then stopped. "I forgot to ask if any of you got the family picture we took on the cruise? Monica said she would have copies made for everyone."

A painful ache pierced Indina's chest at just the mention of the cruise. She shook her head. "Not yet. I'll have to ask Monica."

Although that picture wasn't high on the list of things she wanted sitting on her mantle. The thought of passing it every day and seeing Griffin's smiling face filled her with enough sadness to drown her.

It had been over a week since they

disembarked the ship, and over a week since she'd talked to Griffin.

By the time she woke the morning following their argument, Griffin had already showered and left the cabin. He joined the family at the farewell breakfast aboard the ship, but other than a brusque hello when she sat next to him at breakfast and an even brusquer goodbye once they arrived at the port, he hadn't spoken to her.

Indina had known he was upset, which was why she'd steered clear, hoping to give him the space he needed before attempting to patch things up. She'd considered going over to his house last Monday night, but instead decided to wait until she saw him at work the following day.

But when she arrived at Sykes-Wilcox the next morning, Indina discovered that Griffin had been called to work out of the company's Baton Rouge offices. He remained there for the rest of the week, not returning to the New Orleans office until yesterday morning. Indina still wasn't sure if he'd actively avoided seeing her yesterday or if he just happened not to be around for the few hours she was there.

She'd made every excuse she could think of to explain why she'd been in such a funk since leaving that cruise ship, but deep down Indina knew the truth. She'd been miserable because of how she'd left things with Griffin.

This is why I gave up on relationships.

This shit was just way too complicated.

But the more she thought about it, the more Indina had come to realize that it wasn't complicated at all. She missed him. It was as simple as that.

And it wasn't just about the sex. She missed *Griffin*. She missed the easy conversation they had when she walked into his office at work and perched on the edge of his desk. She missed having someone in her corner, someone she could bounce ideas off of, or complain to when she ran into a roadblock.

When she wasn't thinking about what she missed, she was thinking about what she could have if only she would allow it to happen. She'd gotten a glimpse of it back on that cruise ship. The hours they'd spent talking out on the veranda, holding hands on the beach, lying together all night in bed. That could be her life if she stopped getting in her own way.

She was ready to make that happen. For so long, the thought of placing her heart in someone else's care had scared her to no end. But Indina knew now that she was willing to take that chance.

She was ready to trust Griffin with her heart.

She stood up so abruptly that her chair nearly tumbled to the floor.

"Watch yourself there, Baby Girl," her dad said.

"Sorry. I've got it," Indina said, righting the chair and pushing it under the table. "Are we done here?"

"I guess." Reid shrugged as he shoved a piece of cake into his mouth.

She rounded the table and kissed her dad on the cheek. "I'll be here for dinner on Sunday."

"No, we're going to Margo's, remember?" he said. "They're having a picnic."

"They changed the picnic to Alex and Renee's," Reid said.

"Okay then. I'll see you all at Alex and Renee's."

She loved her family, but she had something else she needed to take care of.

There was a man that she could see herself falling in love with—growing old with—and she had to make sure she hadn't messed things up completely with him. She'd told herself she was done chasing after love, but if it was Griffin's love that awaited her at the end, she was willing to do a bit more chasing.

Griffin picked up his sketch pencil and tapped it against the blotter before tossing it on his desk. He'd started out using the new drafting program the office had recently switched to, but his work had been for shit. He thought going old school with a pencil and paper could possibly shake him out of his funk, but his brain just was not up for design work today.

His brain hadn't been in the mood for working at all lately, which didn't bode well for the project he'd been handed from the Baton Rouge office. Griffin grabbed the pencil again, but just as quickly set it back down. He perched his elbows on his desk and ran his hands down his face.

It didn't matter how much he tried to distract himself with work, or TV, or any of the other methods he'd attempted in the past week, he couldn't get Indina off his mind. How in the hell was he supposed to work when what she'd said to him out on that veranda kept replaying over and over again in his mind?

If I'd known this is what would come of this weekend I never would have invited you to come on this cruise.

The mental torture those words inflicted was worse than anything he'd endured, even during the worst moments of his marriage to Jacqueline. That's how he knew his feelings for Indina ran so much deeper than even he had realized. He'd spent the past week vacillating between cursing himself for pushing her, and being just as upset that he'd waited so long to tell her how he really felt.

Griffin knew he ran the risk of scaring her away. He knew if Indina wasn't ready to take that next step, he could lose her. He'd come to the point where he was willing to take that risk. He just hadn't considered how much it would hurt.

It hurt *so* damn much.

He'd been in agony for over a week, but

Griffin knew the agony would have lasted a lot longer if he had kept his feelings bottled in. He couldn't stomach the thought of going on the way they had been, not after the time he and Indina had spent on that cruise ship. Not after getting to know her and her family. It would have hurt more to return home and only have a part of her, especially after getting a taste of what his life could be like if Indina gave him all of her heart.

And yet, Griffin had lost count of the number of times he'd had to stop himself from calling her and begging for any little crumb she was willing to give him. He'd had to turn off the sound on his text messages after he realized he was damn near getting anxiety attacks every time a text came through, hoping, praying it was from Indina.

But none of them had been from her. He hadn't heard a peep from her since they said their lackluster goodbye at the port once they arrived back in New Orleans. This same woman he'd made love to at least once a week for the past eight months hadn't reached out to him even once since their return.

And that's what hurt him more than anything. How could she just move on after all the time they'd spent together?

"Shit."

Griffin massaged the back of his neck. He had to shake himself out of this. He couldn't go on mired down in this funk he'd found himself in since he stepped off that boat.

His phone vibrated and he nearly knocked over a cup of pens in his haste to reach it. The stupid burst of hope he experienced at the possibility of it being Indina deflated when he realized it wasn't her. But a smile still drew across his lips as he opened the text message from his brother. It was a picture of his nephew in a baseball uniform with the news that he'd made the team at his junior high school.

That was one good thing that had come of the cruise. Being with the Holmes family over the course of those three days had driven home just how much Griffin missed his own family.

Last week, while making the hour and a half long drive back from Baton Rouge, he'd pulled up Garland's contact on his cell phone and made a call that was several years overdue. When his first attempt went to voicemail, Griffin figured his brother wasn't ready to mend fences. But just as he'd tossed it on his passenger seat, his phone rang, with Garland on the other end of the line.

They talked for Griffin's entire ride home. Once he pulled into his driveway, he sat in his car for another hour, trying to cram everything he'd missed over the past two years into a two-hour phone call.

Over this past week, he and Garland had either talked or texted every single day. The two had caught up on everything that had been going on in each other's lives, and Griffin had invited his brother to bring the entire family down to New Orleans sometime in the fall. He still couldn't believe he'd allowed his ex-wife to come between them for so long. He would never make that kind of mistake again.

Griffin didn't miss the irony that it was at Indina's urging that he'd worked out things with his brother, yet he'd blown up everything with her.

How was he supposed to act the first time he saw her again? As if the last week had never happened? Or worse, as if the past eight *months* hadn't?

"No." Griffin shook his head.

He wouldn't do that. He *couldn't*. There was no way in hell he could forget about the time he'd spent with Indina. No way he would throw away the future they could potentially have together.

Indina could argue all she wanted that sex was the only thing they had going for them, but those three days on that cruise proved her wrong. They may have started out as coworkers with benefits, but there was so much more between them. They had the potential to grow their relationship into something that would last, if only he could convince Indina to see that it was worth fighting for.

The doorbell rang just as Griffin picked his phone up to call her.

"Dammit," he cursed as he made his way to the front door. Probably the repairman who was supposed to work on his stove. He'd forgotten to call and cancel the technician after fixing it himself.

Griffin opened the door, preparing to tell the technician he could leave, when the sight before him stopped him cold.

Indina stood on his top step. Her light brown eyes brimmed with regret and the subtle misery Griffin had recognized in his own eyes every time he'd looked in a mirror this past week.

"Hey," she said, a timorous quiver in her voice.

"Hey," he returned.

She cleared her throat. "Do you mind if I come in?"

He opened the door wider and motioned for her to enter.

She walked into the house but didn't go past the foyer. She turned to him, and after a deep breath, said, "I don't even know where to start. An apology maybe?"

Griffin swallowed past the lump that had instantly formed in his throat. "What are you apologizing for?"

"Because I hurt you," she said. "And that is the last thing I ever wanted to do, Griffin. What I said on the veranda that night was callous and wrong. I gave you the impression that I was sorry that you joined me on the cruise, when nothing could be further from the truth."

Even as relief threatened to bring him to his knees, he couldn't help the cautiousness that continued to beat throughout his bloodstream. Why hadn't she called him? Why had she stayed away all week?

"When I didn't hear from you this week, I thought you'd decided that you were done," Griffin said.

"I knew you were upset," she said. "I was trying to give you space."

He stepped up to her. "I don't want space, Indina. I want *you*." He took her hands in his. "Look, we both have our baggage. I allowed what happened with my ex-wife to color my thoughts on relationships for so long that I couldn't recognize a good thing when I was staring directly at it."

"I did the same thing," she said. "I wouldn't allow myself to get too close to you. My body? Yes. But this?" She placed a hand over her heart. "I was too afraid to leave it unguarded, Griffin. It's been broken one too many times. I wasn't willing to take that chance."

He glided his fingers along her cheek in a gentle caress. "Are you willing to take it now?"

Her eyes fell closed as she leaned her face into his palm. The air grew thick as she remained silent. Finally, she opened her eyes and looked up at him.

"I am," she whispered. "I'm willing to trust you with my heart. It scares me, Griffin. It scares me *so* much." She covered the hand that rested on her face, turn her head and kissed the center of his palm. "The only thing that scares me more is the thought of going the rest of my life feeling as miserable as I've felt this past week. This week gave me a glimpse of what my life would be like without you in it. There's nothing that could be worse than that."

The sweetest relief blossomed in his chest. It was so strong he ached with it. Griffin cupped Indina's face in both hands and tilted his head forward until their foreheads met.

"I started falling in love with you months ago, Indina. I tried not to, because I knew it wasn't what you wanted. But every single day the feeling just grew stronger and stronger." He pressed a gentle kiss to her quivering lips. "All I ask is that you give this a chance, a *real* chance. Let me inside your heart. I promise you I'll handle it with care."

He kissed her again. Long and slow and lasting. He kissed her as if it was the last time he would ever get the chance to do it, and sensed his heart expanding with gratitude at the knowledge that this was only the beginning.

Griffin felt Indina's mouth stretch into a smile beneath his lips. He pulled away slightly and asked, "What's so funny?"

Her smile flourished into a thing of beauty. "Just when I thought I was done chasing love, it found me."

"Yes, it did," he said. He drew her into his arms. "And it's never letting you go."

Epilogue

The distinct smell of charcoal and pecan wood imbued the air as the Holmes family gathered in Alex and Renee's huge backyard for yet another gathering. Indina had spent the first half hour fielding questions from the women in her family who wanted to know if Griffin's presence at a second Holmes family function meant their relationship had progressed to more than just coworkers with benefits. Indina could still feel herself blushing as she confirmed their suspicions.

To say he fit right in with her family was an understatement. He'd known them for less than a week, yet Griffin seemed more comfortable than any of her previous boyfriends, even the two she'd dated for several years. It was still much too soon to even consider what their next steps would be, but Indina knew her family was already rooting for her and Griffin to make a trip down the aisle. Renee had revealed as much when she admitted there was a betting pool on where the wedding would take place. Most thought another cruise would be ideal.

Indina wasn't ready to think that far ahead, but she couldn't help the excited tingle that ran through her at the thought of a wedding on the top deck, or maybe even that beautiful private beach in Mexico.

Watch it, girl. You're getting ahead of yourself.

Yet, when Griffin looked over at her and winked, she thought maybe it wasn't so far-fetched.

The picnic soon evolved into a full-on party. Indina doubled over with laughter as she watched Griffin being passed around from one Holmes woman to another. It started with her Aunt Margo, who pulled him up to dance with her when an old O'Jay's song came through the speakers. Monica was next, cajoling him to join in as Liliana taught them some new dance move that was all the rage on YouTube. Even Willow, who for once seemed to be enjoying herself, hopped out of her seat when it was time to do the electric slide.

Indina didn't think she could feel any more content…until she spotted her dad's smiling face. Her chest nearly burst with joy at the sight of him looking so happy.

"Hey, come over here. It's Uncle Toby and Auntie Sienna," Jasmine called. All twenty-plus of them gathered around the table as Jasmine held up her iPad. It didn't matter that they'd all been to the hospital yesterday when Sienna gave birth to Baby Jonah.

Indina's heart squeezed as she watched the sweet baby resting peacefully in Toby's arms. "I'm sorry you two have to miss this," Margo said. "But at least we have a christening to look forward to."

"Somebody's going to bring me a plate, right?" Toby asked.

"I'll be at the hospital this afternoon," Eli said. "I'll bring it."

Sienna, who had been playing camerawoman, flipped the phone's camera to her face. "See how he's just worried about himself?" she said. "You'd better bring two plates, Eli."

Eli gave her a salute. "Aye, Captain."

Sienna and Toby signed off once the baby woke for his feeding, and Reid cranked the music back up.

Indina noticed the uniformed police officer the moment he entered through the wooden gate that led from Alex and Renee's front yard.

"What in the—" Indina set her drink down and followed him.

The music stopped as the officer approached the table where her brothers and cousins were playing dominoes.

"Ezra Holmes?" he asked.

Ezra stood. "I'm Ezra Holmes."

The police officer walked around her brother and pulled his hands behind his back. "You are being arrested for violation of penal code 14.20.2 under the Louisiana state law."

"*What?*" Ezra squawked.

A collective gasp traveled across the backyard as the officer began to read Ezra his Miranda Rights.

"What's going on here?" her dad asked.

"Yes, what is this about?" Indina piped in.

"I have it on good authority that Mr. Holmes has been stalking Councilmember Mackenna Arnold," the officer stated. "You need to come with me."

"Oh, good Lord," Indina said. "Dammit, Ezra, I told you to leave Mack alone. Which station are you taking him to?" she asked the officer as she pulled up Mackenna's number. Her friend didn't pick up. "Dammit," Indina curse. "I'll be at the station in just a few minutes, Ezra."

She headed for the house to get her purse, but Griffin was already standing with it.

"Well, at least I know there will never be a dull moment with the Holmeses," he said as he handed it to her.

Indina couldn't help but laugh. "Welcome to the family."

Thank you so much for purchasing and reading *Chase Me*. If you haven't read them yet, be sure to check out the original Holmes Brothers, and on the lookout for *Trust Me*, Ezra and Mackenna's story!

The Holmes Brother Series:

Set in New Orleans, the Holmes Brothers series follows the lives of Elijah, Tobias, and Alexander Holmes as they find love in one of the world's most romantic cities.

Read ***Deliver Me***, ***Release Me***, and ***Rescue Me***!

Moments in Maplesville

A Perfect Holiday Fling (Callie & Stefan)
A Little Bit Naughty (Jada & Mason)
Just a Little Taste (Kiera & Trey)
I Dare You! (Stephanie & Dustin)
All You Can Handle (Sonny & Ian)
Any Way You Want It (Nyree & Dale)
Any Time You Need Me (Aubrey & Sam)

*Find a list of all of my books at
www.farrahrochon.com.*

About the Author:

USA Today Bestselling author Farrah Rochon hails from a small town just west of New Orleans. She has garnered much acclaim for her Holmes Brothers, New York Sabers, Bayou Dreams and Moments in Maplesville series. *I'll Catch You*, the second book in her New York Sabers series for Harlequin Kimani, was a 2012 RITA ® Award finalist. Yours Forever, the third book in the Bayou Dreams series, was a 2015 RITA® Award finalist. Farrah has been nominated for an RT BOOKReviews Reviewers Choice Award, and in 2015 received the Emma Award for Author of the Year.

When she is not writing in her favorite coffee shop, Farrah spends most of her time reading her favorite romance novels or seeing as many Broadway shows as possible. An admitted sports fanatic, Farrah feeds her addiction to football by watching New Orleans Saints games on Sunday afternoons.

Made in the USA
Middletown, DE
11 August 2017